ENDLESS ORDEAL

A WEHRMACHT SOLDIER IN RUSSIAN CAPTIVITY

MARION KUMMEROW

Endless Ordeal, An Unforgettable and Fast-Paced WWII Novel

War Girls Series, Book 11

Marion Kummerow

ISBN Paperback 978-3-948865-21-4

All Rights Reserved

Copyright © 2019 Marion Kummerow

This book is copyrighted and protected by copyright laws.

No part of this publication may be reproduced or transmitted in any form or by any means, electronic, mechanical, photocopying, recording, or otherwise without prior written permission from the author.

This is a work of fiction. All characters, names, and places in this book exist only within the author's imagination. Any resemblance to actual persons or locations is purely coincidental.

Cover Design by http://www.StunningBookCovers.com

READER GROUP

Marion's Reader Group

Sign up for my reader group to receive exclusive background information and be the first one to know when a new book is released.

http://kummerow.info/subscribe

CHAPTER 1

January 1945, Warsaw, Poland

Johann stared into the muzzle of a Mosin Nagant pointed at his face. The man at the other end of the gun was a Red Army soldier, who looked as filthy and exhausted as Johann felt.

"Surrender! Hands up!" the Russian shouted in broken German, and, after a short glimpse out of the corner of his eye, Johann obeyed.

It was senseless to fight, since left and right all his comrades were in the exact same situation. Raising his hands above his head, Johann met the eyes of the Russian, and the realization hit him square in the chest.

My war is over. No more fighting. No more killing.

The Russian beckoned at him to hand over his weapon and move to where an entire column of Wehrmacht soldiers had been herded together. As Johann turned in his trusted MG34 to the soldier who'd captured him, a wave of relief washed over his body, closely followed by terror. He had survived the fighting; now what?

The rumors and stories about the Red Army weren't the stuff to ease worries and calm fears. In fact, the Wehrmacht soldiers had invented a particular word for the terrors that being captured by the Russians evoked: *Russenschreck*.

One of the common pieces of wisdom dictated that the Russians didn't take prisoners. Johann swallowed and walked toward his comrades, fully expecting a bullet in the back of his head at any moment. But nothing happened.

The young men posted to guard the new prisoners of war seemed as relieved as he was to have survived the battle for Warsaw and made no move to kill their former opponents. Some even smiled and started a conversation.

Johann, though, didn't speak Russian and preferred to stay away from the guards, just in case. He meandered to the center of the group and finally came upon someone he knew.

"Helmut!"

His longtime comrade turned around and looked at him with bleak eyes. "Johann. You got water?"

Johann handed him his canteen. "Been here for long?"

"Two days. No food, no water. Just the snow to lick, but that's gone now, too."

"What are they going to do with us?"

"No idea." Helmut handed him back the canteen. "Looks like they don't know themselves." He nodded at one of the Soviet officers, a short man with a fur hat and a long khaki coat with red lapels. "Seems he's the one in charge, but as clueless as the rest."

That didn't sound encouraging. Johann hoped they'd soon make up their minds and wouldn't keep them rotting out there, exposed to wind and snow. A commotion at the other end of the group drew his attention. Russian soldiers were going prisoner by prisoner, doing something.

"Stealing valuables," Helmut said. "They're nuts for watches, but will take anything of value you have."

Moments later, one of the Red Army soldiers approached him and said, "Watch!"

Johann looked at his army-issue wristwatch. It was neither beautiful nor valuable, but it reliably told him the time. He'd miss it.

He removed his watch and gave it to the man, who slipped it onto his right wrist, since the left one already featured three watches.

"Metals."

Johann squinted at the other man, unsure what he wanted.

"He wants your insignia and medals," Helmut explained.

Scanning his friend's body, Johann realized that Helmut's own uniform was bare of any signs of rank that could easily be yanked off.

Well, they wouldn't be of much use anymore. He removed his epaulets and put them into the outstretched hand of the Russian.

"Belt," the man demanded.

Johann looked down at the leather belt with the metal buckle that said *Gott mit uns*, God with us. The Russian didn't like this moment of hesitation and pointed his rifle at Johann. "Fast."

"Yes." He nodded, his fingers moving to open the buckle and remove the belt. His trousers instantly slipped down to his hips, before the suspenders held them up.

The Russian seemed content with his booty and walked to the next prisoner. Johann gave a big, yet silent, sigh. He was still alive. Deprived of all his valuables, but alive.

At least he still had his canteen, pen and a notepad, his girlfriend Lotte's photograph, cutlery, a piece of bread, and his knapsack with extra underwear, socks, and toiletries.

And his *Soldbuch*. If the Russians allowed them to maintain the booklet that served as documentation and pay book, they might indeed intend to keep them alive and take them prisoners.

His exhausted legs wobbled and Johann wanted to slump down on the ground, but the half-frozen mud didn't look appealing. The ice would only melt beneath him, soaking into his trousers and letting the cold creep into his bones.

No, it was preferable to stand.

The next day, a vehicle arrived with some important looking Soviet officers. They conferred for a while and then beckoned at some of the ranks to distribute stacks of something white.

Johann eyed them curiously, hoping for something to eat, but it turned out to be white strips of fabric, each approximately seven by ten inches in size with the Cyrillic letters W and P stamped on them.

"That means *voyennoplenny*, Russian for prisoner of war," a helpful comrade explained.

The Russian soldier pointed to Johann's left sleeve and Johann tied the strip of cloth over his jacket, just above his left elbow. It was only a piece of cloth, but it felt like a heavy burden. Degradation. He wasn't Leutnant Hauser anymore, but simply part of the ever-growing anonymous mass of POWs.

Once all of the men had received this new identifier, someone gave the command to march. Still hopeful for food, Johann joined the line. As he passed a destroyed house, he reached out his hand to snatch some snow from the top of a wall, only to feel the stabbing pain of a rifle butt coming down on his arm.

"Walk!"

Johann quickly retracted his hand, holding onto a bit of snow. He waited until the guard slipped from sight and shoved the melting ice into his mouth. It was barely enough to moisten his dry mouth, with only a few drops left to swallow.

After marching for approximately an hour, the Russians ushered them into a fenced-off area where already hundreds of miserable, dejected, dirty, crazy-eyed and bald Wehrmacht soldiers slumped on the bare tarmac.

Guards distributed hair clippers to the newcomers and indicated they were to shave one another's heads completely bald.

Johann stared at Helmut, who had some rudimentary knowledge of Russian. "What's this all about?"

Helmut shrugged. "No idea. Our captors aren't exactly

generous with explanations. We better do what they want, though."

"Who's first?" Johann asked.

"You shave me, of course. Then I can avenge any cuts you should give me."

"Oh, nice, stabbing your friend in the back."

Helmut lowered his head so Johann could start shaving – without water or foam – and mumbled, "If what they say is true, we soon won't have the luxury of friends, and it's every man for himself."

Johann started scratching away at Helmut's blond hair with the blunt clippers and pondered his friend's words. Was having a friend a luxury and was it true that a captive soldier was better off by himself? He didn't think so, but what did he know about surviving in captivity?

Nothing.

"Done. You look awful," he said to Helmut and handed him the clippers to return the favor.

"And it's awfully cold," Helmut answered even as he started shaving Johann's head.

Helmut was right. As soon as the strands of his light brown hair fell to his shoulders, an icy gust hit Johann's head. The Russians had taken their helmets earlier, but he hoped they'd at least leave them the forage caps to protect their heads from the Polish winter.

More commands were bellowed through the air in a peculiar mixture of Russian and German, but the meaning was clear. Everyone line up for personal search.

Johann sighed. They'd searched him twice already. What did they expect he was hiding? There seemed to be no real sense nor reason to their intentions, because the Russians took away Helmut's cutlery, but left Johann's and took his woolen socks instead.

Perhaps it was simply a means to replenish whatever equipment the searching soldier was currently lacking. An officer walked from man to man, scrutinizing their lapels and seemingly at random picking prisoners from the line and sending them to the other side of the fenced-off area.

Johann's spirits fell and his earlier hope began to dwindle as the officer made his way to him and Helmut. More and more prisoners were sent to the other side. He didn't comprehend the selection process, didn't even know whether it was better to stay on this side or to be sent to the other one. Never a religious person, he suddenly had the urge to send a prayer to God. *Please, let me stay alive.*

The officer reached Helmut and gave him a surprisingly friendly nod, asking for his *Soldbuch*. "*Gut. Gut.*" He took the booklet and returned it. "This is your documentation. Keep it safe." Then he walked further down the line – and disappeared from sight.

"What now?" Johann asked.

"No idea."

So they waited. Some of their comrades stepped out of the line to scrounge for scraps of snow to quench their thirst. Nobody killed, beat, or harangued them. Emboldened by the non-reaction of their captors, more and more prisoners did the same until they'd licked up the last trace of snow and ice.

"In line," someone bellowed, and the prisoners hurried to form a queue. Another group of Russians came, making yet another body search. This time they only took the

Soldbücher and tossed them onto a big pile in the middle of the fenced-off area.

Johann's heart dropped to his feet. The Russian officer had told them to keep it safe, for it was their documentation. Had they changed their minds and would now kill them all?

His eyes widened in shock when he observed how a Russian soldier set fire to the pile. All his hopes went up in smoke along with the identification papers. Renewed dread filled his soul.

At least the fire brought some warmth into the air and he inched nearer to melt his frozen limbs. Staring into the dancing flames, sadness engulfed him. So this was the culmination of his life?

He was twenty-nine years old and had learned nothing but how to be a soldier. Initially, he had joined the Wehrmacht and later the Party, because he was fascinated by Hitler's promise to repeal the unjust Versailles Treaty. Make Germany great again. But Hitler's atrocious persecution of the Jews and other groups of people had soon put a damper on his enthusiasm.

Shamefully, Johann admitted to himself that he'd been deluded to believe the Jews were the main cause for the moribund condition Germany had fallen into after the Great War. But even if Hitler's machinations were true – and he seriously doubted that in the meantime – the Jews hadn't deserved the disgusting treatment. No human being deserved to be persecuted, tortured and obliterated from the face of earth.

"Everyone over there!" The command penetrated his thoughts, whisking away the guilt and self-pity he felt.

Johann queued up behind Helmut and waited, his breath stalling in his lungs. After an agonizing wait he reached the head of the line and found himself standing in front of a long table with numerous Red Army soldiers sitting behind, scribbling notes on long lists.

"Name?" the soldier demanded.

"Johann Hauser."

"Father's first name?"

What on earth does he need that for? But he didn't dare ask questions and said, "Hans."

"Year?"

Johann gave the soldier a puzzled look. "I don't understand."

"Year of birth?" the soldier said, growing angry at having to repeat himself.

"1916."

"Place?"

"Munich, Germany."

The soldier whisked him forward and Johann wondered why they had destroyed the *Soldbücher*. It would have been much more practical to take the required information from the document than to ask each prisoner to provide it.

He turned his head to the left and saw two SS men hurriedly yanking off their insignia before it became their turn to register. With their *Soldbücher* destroyed, those who had something to hide could easily lie during the registration process. Johann hated what he viewed as betrayal, but given the horrible stories circulating about the special treatment the Red Army doled out to members of the SS, he could somehow understand it.

The next day more than a thousand prisoners were

marched to an engineers' bridge across the Vistula and into a farmstead. Here they were finally given food – bread and soup. The meager rations didn't still his hunger, but at least the soup quenched the agonizing thirst. Next, everyone was ordered into the courtyard for roll call.

It was a peculiar sight to see the members of the formerly proud, even invincible Wehrmacht, standing there, dejected and desolate.

"What do they want now?" he whispered to Helmut, who only shook his head.

"A brighter man than me is needed to understand the Russian mind."

That much was true. So far, none of the actions of their captors had been predictable or comprehensible.

A Soviet officer stepped forward and asked in English, "Any British or American nationals present?"

Two men in RAF uniforms stepped forward and Johann wondered how on earth they'd managed to be captured along with the Germans. The two Englishmen were immediately whisked away to meet the commandant.

"Frenchmen?"

Dozens of men in Wehrmacht uniform stepped forward, identifying themselves as *malgré-nous*, men of the Alsace-Lorraine region who had been forcefully conscripted into the Wehrmacht.

"Come on. That fellow is as much French as I am Russian," Helmut mumbled at the sight of a short, dark-haired soldier. "He's from the Saarland."

"To each his own," Johann mumbled back. Confronted with the overwhelming horror of the *Russenschreck*, who could hold it against the man for trying to evade captivity?

On and on it went. Poles, Czechs, Yugoslavs, Romanians, Bulgarians, even Austrians stepped forward and were counted. But much to their dismay everyone who wore the German uniform had to step back into the line, independent of their true or alleged nationality. Only the men wearing an Allied uniform were released.

CHAPTER 2

J ohann had already spent two weeks on the farmstead and each day more prisoners arrived. According to the Soviets, this was only a temporary camp to collect prisoners and then send them onward to a real camp.

But since the Red Army was still fighting their way to Berlin, they understandably had more pressing issues than a bunch of bedraggled enemy combatants. The guards inhabited the ruins of the bombed-out buildings while the POWs had to stay out in the open, exposed to wind and weather.

A bone-numbing cold seeped into every cell in Johann's body ever since the day he was taken captive. The frozen limbs and deep-frozen bones served as constant companion, along with the nagging hunger. Their captors provided them with a thin soup and bread once a day, but it was never enough. Especially because more and more soldiers poured into the small area, competing for space and food. At least the drizzling snow could be used to quench the maddening thirst.

Another problem was the boredom – and the worrisome thoughts that came with it. With nothing else to occupy his hands or his mind, Johann constantly worried.

About himself and his future. About his parents. About his friends. But mostly about Lotte. The last time he'd seen her was half a year earlier in Warsaw, when he'd put her on a train to Berlin together with her friend, Gerlinde, and her nephew, Jan.

Lotte worked as a radio operator for the Wehrmacht and had been posted to Stavanger in Norway. He should be pleased, because he'd personally had a hand in her latest posting. Stavanger was by far one of the safest places to stay during this war. Sure, the fighting after the invasion had been fierce – for a month. Since then, nothing much had happened in Norway, unlike in the more violent theaters like Poland, where he'd met her.

He touched her letter in his breast pocket, but his fingers were too nearly frozen stiff to take it out. It didn't matter, because he knew its contents by heart from reading it several dozen times.

His mind drifted away to last summer in Warsaw, and the oppressive heat he'd welcome with open arms right now. He'd fancied the fierce and spunky redhead at first sight, because she was so different from everyone else.

Much later he'd found out just how different she really was… but by then he'd fallen head over heels for her already and would have given his right arm to protect her. Thankfully, it hadn't come to that extreme. Although he'd had to lie, steal, and deceive to keep her alive.

"I don't know if I'll ever feel warm again," his neighbor's voice broke into his musings. The prisoners huddled in a tight circle, their backs to the icy breeze coming from the east.

Johann lifted his hands to his chapped lips and blew into them. "How much longer are they going to keep us out here? I wish they'd just send us to wherever our destination is."

Helmut gave a sarcastic laugh. "Be careful what you wish for."

"It can't really get much worse."

"You have no idea. If only one tenth of the rumors are true, we're in for an awful surprise."

"We should try to escape," another soldier, called Heinz, said.

"Escape? And where would you go?" asked Johann.

"Somewhere. Anywhere but here." Heinz rubbed the icicles from his nose.

"He's right. They don't have many guards and there's not even a fence around this place," another man chimed in.

Glancing around, Johann admitted the truth in the man's words. The Soviets used only about a dozen armed soldiers to guard a thousand prisoners. But they didn't hesitate to shoot anyone trying to escape. With nowhere to hide, a fleeing man in his *feldgrau* uniform could be seen for miles against the white landscape.

Even if a prisoner made it, where would he go? The Polish population wasn't exactly fond of the former oppressors and would rather lynch a Wehrmacht soldier than help him escape the Russians.

"Be my guest. Make your move," Johann said and gazed across the sorry bunch of huddled men. Most were too injured, too sick, or too malnourished to even think of running. For a week now dysentery had been ravaging the camp, depleting the men's ability to withstand the harsh conditions.

Every morning the prisoners dragged more corpses to the far side of the field and tossed them into deep open pits. With each passing day the pits filled faster, soon outpacing the speed with which the prisoners could dig out new ones in the frozen earth.

A murmur went through the crowd as several trucks with Red Army soldiers arrived.

"What's happening?" Heinz asked.

"No idea," Johann said. They'd find out soon enough.

"Everyone line up!" The barked order caused the bedraggled crowd of men to stumble into something akin to a line.

Another search? Johann inwardly groaned. He kept close to Helmut, even reached for his arm to prevent them from being separated. Whatever was happening he didn't want to face it without his only friend. Heinz clung to them, as did Karl, and the four of them managed to stay together.

The Soviets counted batches of five hundred prisoners and one batch after another was marched out of the camp. When it was their turn to leave, a wave of nostalgia swept over Johann. As bad as conditions had been, at least the camp was familiar by now.

Anything else was uncertain. He knew neither where they were headed nor what awaited them there. And the Russians weren't inclined to explain. Only after marching half a day, someone snapped up a conversation between two guards and the news spread like wildfire through the column. "We're being transferred to Plonsk."

"That's about fifty miles northwest. Does that mean they plan on sending us home?" Helmut asked.

"That would be outright stupid of them, because the war's still on." Johann shook his head. The more probable explanation was they had liberated Soviet POWs from a Wehrmacht camp and were now reusing the same facilities to hold their own prisoners.

What concerned him more was the fact that Plonsk was a good three-day march away. The Russians didn't genuinely expect the debilitated men to walk the entire distance?

He soon found out that they did.

Johann, Helmut, Heinz and Karl walked side by side from sunup to sundown, with little to no food, no water, and unpredictable winter weather upon them. When one of them stumbled, the others would drag that man up again, for the Russian guards didn't exercise much patience with those who couldn't keep up the pace.

Johann soon saw the futility of worrying about hunger, cold and pain, and exclusively focused on setting one foot in front of the other. Step by step inching in the direction of Plonsk. But not even the prospect of returning to Germany one day could raise his spirits.

He succumbed to his delirious pains, until the sight of a comrade lying in the snow shook him from his apathy. The man's pale face blended into the snow and for a moment Johann thought the dreadful march might be a blessing in disguise. If their guards didn't force them to keep walking, the prisoners would rest in the snow and ultimately end up frozen into eternity.

The squishing sound of his soaked leather boots formed

a melody and Johann steadied the rhythm of his steps. Short squish with the left foot, longer one with the right foot. His feet were frozen solid in the shoes, so he didn't feel the pain of the forming blisters that undoubtedly would tear open to form ghastly wounds.

On the second day he could no longer summon the will to care. During his few lucid moments Johann wondered whether he was even alive or if this was some kind of purgatory where he had to atone for his sins.

The temperature had fallen constantly during the past days, and after a night huddled together in the snow, dozens of men simply wouldn't wake up anymore. He cast a glance at their angelical faces, peaceful at last, devoid of hunger and pain. And for a fleeting moment he wished to follow them to wherever they were. Only the thought of soft and warm Lotte wrapped in his arms, pressing a passionate kiss on his lips, sent some much-needed heat into his bones and kept a tiny flicker of life burning inside him.

He slipped. The earth welcomed him, beckoned at him to lie down and relax. A ray of sunshine hit his face, making him smile. Everything would be alright. There was no pain. No sorrow.

Nothing.

"Get up," one of the guards shouted.

Helmut slapped Johann's cheek and somehow shoved him upward. For a moment, Johann wanted to yell at his friend for making him leave the peaceful place. But then he glimpsed reality and struggled to a stand, staggering forward with Helmut's help.

Hours later he was still marching, unsure whether to thank his friend or curse him for not letting him die back there. It would have been so easy. Close his eyes and succumb to a peaceful sleep, never to wake up again.

The crowd of men trudging along continued to dwindle. By noon the sun stood high enough for Johann to feel her warming rays – not enough to heat up the air, but at least melting the ice on his uniform.

Over time the march became even more tedious and he couldn't explain why, not until he raised his head and saw they were walking up a hill. The pace of the weakened prisoners slowed down. He continued to struggle on. Minute after minute. Yard after yard. Step after step.

God, I wish this horrific ordeal would just end.

Two men in front of him slipped on the treacherous slope and fell, tumbling a short distance off the pathway. The guards rushed toward them with raised rifles, yelling at them to get up.

"My ankle… I think it's broken," one of the men gasped, even as his comrade somehow stumbled to his feet, shoved forward by the guard.

Johann watched helplessly how the injured man struggled to get to his feet, but instantly fell down again. After two attempts, one of the guards took a step back, and discharged a bullet into the head of the fallen man.

Anger rose in Johann's chest, pushing the apathy aside, and he clenched his fists as hatred for the Russian guards filled his soul. His muscles tightened and he vibrated with the need to seek justice for the now dead man.

"It's not worth your life." Helmut held his arm.

Johann swallowed hard as emotions flooded his body, but under Helmut's unforgiving grip he couldn't do anything other than continue on his march. Only his mind stayed behind with the dead prisoner left to rot alongside the trail. Images of the young man's family back home, a sweetheart desperately waiting for news of her man attacked him, clawing at his heart and soul and he wished he'd at least known the soldier's name to somehow inform them of his fate.

For the next few hours, Johann's anger fueled his march, heated his body, and at the end of the day he was even more exhausted than usual. The emotional turmoil roiling within him had taken its toll.

"You need to calm down," Helmut said.

"I'm calm."

"No, you're not. And it will do you no good." Helmut managed a smile. "If you want to do something, let us say a prayer for the dead men."

"A prayer? How will that help?"

"Everything." Helmut never let anyone ridicule his strong faith in God. He took out a tiny pocket Bible to read the word of the day.

Johann listened begrudgingly to the sermon that followed, but didn't dare to interrupt. Secretly, he wished he had the same faith as Helmut. Whatever hardships were thrown at him, Helmut never fought against them, but accepted their existence and tried to find a way to live with them.

Tolerance was a new experience for Johann, who'd been full of anger throughout most of his life. Anger for the Allies who strangled Germany after the Great War. Anger for the Jews who dealt the fatal blow to his beloved country. Anger for the British bastards who'd framed him in Shanghai and used him as a convenient scapegoat. Anger for the

Wehrmacht who had kept him waiting for a promotion after this incident... and now anger for the Soviets who treated him with such deplorable cruelty.

Three horrendous days after leaving the farmstead, half of the sorry group of bedraggled men arrived at Plonsk. As Johann had suspected it was a former Wehrmacht POW camp that now held tens of thousands of the former masters.

At least there were barracks to shield them from wind and weather, and daily meals. But first, they had to register – again.

The Russians asked him the same question as in Warsaw. His answers were recorded into the same type of lists, and Johann began to suspect that those lists from Warsaw had never made it here.

CHAPTER 3

L ife in the camp was harsh, but at least the worst of the winter was over.

"The Ivan has no right to treat us this way," one of the German prisoners complained.

Johann glowered at him but kept his mouth shut. The complainer was a former SS man and only alive because he'd given the captors a false identity, claiming to be an ordinary Wehrmacht soldier.

"Yes, how about the Geneva Convention?" another converted SS man asked.

Johann scoffed and now it was the other men's turn to glower at him. He wanted to give them a piece of his mind, tell them the kind of despicable cowards they were. But he kept his mouth shut, since he didn't want trouble. The Russians never asked who started arguments, but punished both parties indiscriminately.

After some more complaints, Helmut raised his voice

and said, "How can you expect them to treat us better than we treated theirs?"

"That's because they're subhumans. No better than animals. We shouldn't even be here," the SS man growled.

"Right, you shouldn't. You should have a bullet through your head for all the war crimes you committed," Johann muttered beneath his breath.

Most every prisoner in here loathed the former SS men, but nobody would dare to rat them out to the Russian captors. Even the worst of them were still Germans, fellow prisoners, and compatriots. Ratting out a compatriot wasn't something a Wehrmacht soldier did. Ever. It didn't matter how Johann felt about the other man. Their nations were at war and the Russians were the enemy. Full stop. There was nothing to quibble about, despite his personal feelings about it.

Helmut elbowed him and whispered, "Let it go. They'll get what is theirs one day. If not in this world, then during the final judgment."

"Hmm." Johann shook his head. He had no idea how Helmut could still believe in a God of justice. For some strange reason, Helmut derived strength and even contentment amidst the deplorable conditions from reading the word of God.

"Someone should do something," Johann murmured.

"Not your concern."

If he weren't so cold, hungry, and miserable, Johann would at least get angry at the fatalistic behavior of his friend. But instead he leaned back on his elbows and murmured, "They should have to pay for their sins."

"And they will. But it's not your job to seek justice for them."

"How can you be so… so indifferent?" Johann sighed, squinting his eyes against the weak sunshine warming his bones. Deep inside he knew Helmut was right. Collaboration with the Russians was a worse crime than shedding one's SS past to evade execution. The other prisoners would lynch him, should he turn in one of his own kind.

"I think this place is a very fitting punishment for them," Helmut mused after a while.

"And what about us? Do we deserve to be treated like this?"

"God's ways are mysterious, and we should try to find something positive in our situation."

Something positive? In this hellhole? Sometimes Johann doubted Helmut's sanity. Fortunately his own brain was too starved and weak to ponder the greater meaning of his suffering and whether he deserved the punishment doled out by God at the hand of the Russians.

In Johann's book he'd already atoned for all past, present and future sins by rotting away for months in a Chinese prison for a crime he hadn't committed. He mentally scoffed. It was a fate of irony that of all people the only one to believe him had been a Jewess.

A Jewess taking pity on a Nazi.

He wondered what had become of her. Had she made it through the war? Did she still live in Shanghai? He would probably never know, but just in case, he prayed for her to be alive and well.

Several weeks passed and spring returned, bringing with it

warmer temperatures. A quiet desperation settled amongst the prisoners. Several dozen died each night and were thrown on handcarts to be dumped in the mass graves at the far end of the camp. But a bigger number of newcomers each day replaced those who perished, and the camp was bursting at the seams.

"Line up for roll call!" The command bellowed through the loudspeakers.

Johann dreaded the roll calls. Nothing good ever came out of them. Apart from making them stand motionless hour after hour, the Russians usually selected *volunteers* for whatever tedious task had to be done. Sometimes they offered extra food in exchange, but more often than not, it was simply extra work.

"What's going on?" Helmut asked as they fell in line.

"There are rumors of a transfer," said Gerd, who spoke fluent Russian and therefore was usually well-informed.

"Transfer? Someplace where there is more room? More food? A bath?" Johann suggested hopefully.

"Don't get your hopes up," Gerd answered.

The Soviet guards walked along the lines and ordered groups of forty to march toward the exit of the camp. As usual, no explanation was given, and nobody dared to ask. Even if the Russians were in a friendly mood, communication was severely limited by the lack of mutual language skills.

When one of the more accessible guards came to their group, counting down the line from one to forty, Johann elbowed Gerd and whispered, "Ask."

Gerd mustered all his courage and said something in Russian. The guard seemed surprised to have a prisoner speak his native tongue and a short conversation ensued, before the group was marched off.

"What did he say?" Johann was dying of curiosity.

"He said we're being moved to another camp. A better place. In Mother Russia."

"That sounds promising," Helmut said. As always, he was a role model of optimism, refusing to surrender to the hardships thrown at them.

"I don't believe a single word they say, and you shouldn't, either," Gerd said, hurrying to keep pace with the man in front of him as they marched out of the camp.

After about an hour they stopped in front of a train station. An endless cargo train with dozens upon dozens of cattle cars stood on the rails, waiting. The locomotive sent clouds of steam skyward like someone puffing at a cigarette. Johann had never been a heavy smoker, but now he longed for the comfort of a stub.

Batches of prisoners were shoved into the cattle cars and whenever a dozen or so wagons were filled and sealed, the locomotive moved forward. Another dozen carts pulled into the train station, opening their empty bellies to swallow up another bunch of miserable POWs.

The whole scene had a surreal touch to it, and Johann would have laughed if it weren't so drab. He dreaded setting foot inside the train destined for Russia. But any kind of resistance was futile and the only way he'd stay in Plonsk would be as a corpse.

He stuck to Gerd and Helmut, climbing into the car, and hoping that being together with his comrades would bring a modicum of consolation. It was incredibly crowded inside and a few of the men started screaming, as the doors closed, and twilight settled over them.

"How long do you think it'll take?" Johann asked.

"Not more than a few hours, I'm sure," Helmut answered.

Johann couldn't make out the expression on his friend's face, but Helmut's voice was as calm and composed as usual. He clung to the words, hoping Helmut was right.

There wasn't enough room to sit, or lie down, and for lack of ventilation the air soon became thick, fetid and oppressively hot. Fortunately, Gerd's foresight had pushed the three of them against the outer wall. At least every time the train moved along to load new prisoners, a breeze of oxygen hit their noses, reinvigorating their brains and cooling their bodies. After endless hours of waiting, the train finally left Plonsk and huffed and puffed eastward through the Polish plains.

Night fell, dawn rose, and they were still moving at an excruciatingly slow speed, halting every now and then for undisclosed reasons. Given the devastated state of the country, their halts were most likely caused by damaged rails or other obstacles.

Delirious with thirst, his legs cramping, Johann almost wished the Soviets had forced them to march again.

"This one's dead," someone said.

"You sure?"

"Bloody sure I am – there's a fucking corpse leaning on my shoulder."

"Let him fall down," another man suggested.

"And how exactly am I supposed to do that?" the first one sneered. "We're like sardines in a tin."

A short conversation ensued, and one man took it upon himself to coordinate the others. On his command everyone swayed in one direction and the corpse fell to the floor. As more comrades died, the surviving men had more room and settled atop of them. After three days and three nights, the train stopped and the doors opened, the men nearest to the door toppling over and falling outside.

Johann squinted against the blinding sunlight.

"Out! Out!" the guards shouted, and thirty men stumbled outside falling over each other.

Johann spotted a barrel and dragged Helmut and Gerd along, hoping to find some water. The water was stale and filthy, but after three days without a single drop of liquid he didn't care. He scooped the water into his hands and drank greedily, before he was shoved away by other thirsty men.

Someone distributed bread to the prisoners and Johann flopped to the ground carefully chewing the hard, black bread.

"It's a wonderful day," Helmut said, admiring the spring sunshine,

Johann stared at him, aghast. "How can you be so… content? We barely survived that dreadful journey."

Helmut shrugged. "But now we're lying in the sun, a piece of bread in our hands. The sun is shining, and the birds are singing."

"You're positively insane," Johann murmured. "Where are we anyway?"

Gerd glanced around and deciphered the Cyrillic letters on the half-destroyed station building. "Brest-Litowsk. I guess that's why they let us out."

Johann searched his brain and remembered that the

Russian railway system used a broader gauge than the rest of Europe. Brest-Litowsk was the border town between Poland and Belarus where the two different systems met.

Since he didn't expect the Russians to have fancy gauge conversion tools for the cattle cars, the prisoners most probably would be herded into different trains. A cold shiver ran down his spine thinking about another dreadful journey ahead of him.

But then he decided to do as Helmut did and not worry so much. Instead, he relished chewing on his bread and soaking up the sunlight.

Looking back toward the long train that spewed prisoners onto the platform, he noticed that some of the men had been tasked with piling up the corpses and cleaning the cars of feces and other human waste. It seemed Helmut was right, and a silver lining could be found at any time. They hadn't been burdened with that ghastly job.

He must have dozed off, because shouting woke him, and he saw that once again the prisoners had to register. Struggling to his feet, he took up his place in the line. He'd never understand the strange predilection of the Soviets to put everything into lists and then never to consult those lists, but to make new ones with the same information.

"They're asking for occupation. I wonder what for," Helmut remarked.

"Who knows?" Gerd said. "I may understand their language, but I don't have the slightest idea what's going on in their heads."

They observed how the Soviets formed groups of prisoners according to the stated professions.

"I'm guessing they need skilled people for some kind of work," Helmut said.

"Too bad I never learned anything but the trade of a soldier," Johann murmured.

"I'm a carpenter," Gerd said.

"And I'm a master locksmith. Tell them you're one too, when they ask," Helmut offered.

Johann stared at his friend. "But I have no idea about this stuff."

"I'll teach you. It's really not that hard."

When it was Johann's turn to register, he did as Helmut had told him, and much to his surprise, it worked. He was moved to one group with locksmiths, carpenters, brick masons, and electricians, while farmers, bakers, and butchers where moved to a second group, and other professions to a third and fourth group according to some secret master plan.

As night settled trains arrived on the wide-gauge rails and, group after group, the prisoners were shoved into the trains. Before long, Johann heard the locomotive starting up. The wheels clattered along as they gradually gained speed over the metal rails.

This time, the cars were slightly less crowded and, in the middle, stood a huge plastic barrel with water to drink and a much smaller empty bucket in one of the corners to relieve themselves.

There was a tiny window in one of the walls, through which they discarded their dead comrades. Johann flinched every time at the sound of a corpse hitting the gravel and shivered uncontrollably when a body was squashed beneath the wheels of the train. Once the Russians found out about the unconventional burial method, they nailed up the window with a wooden plank.

Now the corpses stayed, befouling the air inside and staring at their living comrades with hollow eyes. Every day or two, the train would stop. The bucket was emptied and the barrel filled. And sometimes loaves of bread were hurled inside.

One week passed and then two. The cattle car was comfortably empty by now and the water barrel actually lasted the entire day. By the time the third week arrived, Johann was sure he'd never leave that cursed train again. The oppressive heat increased exponentially during the day, just to drop below freezing point during the night. The stench was nauseating.

"We've stopped again," Johann murmured to Helmut, who was propped up against the rough boards.

He listened for footfalls, blinking rapidly when the doors slid open a few moments later and Soviet soldiers commanded them to exit the train.

"Seems we have arrived," Johann murmured.

"I don't think I can walk," Helmut said.

Johann wrapped his arm around Helmut's waist and together they stumbled out of the car on wobbly legs. He had no idea where they were, but it probably didn't matter. He just hoped it wasn't Siberia, for he had heard the most awful things about that godforsaken place.

"No ice, so that's good," Helmut said, seemingly having the same thoughts. "I heard there's ice in Siberia all year round."

Gerd staggered behind them, rasping in a rough voice,

"That's a stark exaggeration. There's like six weeks of summer in Siberia."

Usually, Johann would have made some kind of joke, but right now he was too exhausted to utter unnecessary words. He focused on making his legs obey the commands of his brain. The guards were in a hurry to get the prisoners away from the train station to their final destination, and mercilessly pushed them forward.

"Where are we?" Johann murmured, but nobody knew the answer. About an hour later they reached the POW camp. After another registration the *Altgefangene,* the German POWs who'd been here since 1942, filled them in.

"Welcome to Voronezh," the barracks' eldest, Karsten, said.

Karsten looked older than Johann's own grandpa, but it turned out he was barely over thirty. While Johann was considerably shocked at the sight of the emaciated man, Helmut said, "So it is possible to survive three years in Russian captivity."

"I sure hope we won't be here for that long."

CHAPTER 4

T he barracks had windows, but no glass in them. In order to keep the bugs and the weather out, previous prisoners had used paper, rags, and pieces of wood to seal the openings.

When Johann entered his new home, a shudder ran down his spine. He'd seen many depressing sights throughout the war, but this was in a category all of its own.

The barracks was set up with narrow two-tiered bunks on either side with a small aisle between them. He estimated that three hundred men were crammed into the building. The door clicked shut behind him, leaving the interior in almost complete darkness.

Suddenly, he wished he'd died in combat.

Karsten assigned the newcomers bunks. He bared his rotten teeth with an apologetic smile and said, "Sorry, but you'll have to share, at least for tonight."

Helmut elbowed Johann and headed for one of the few

bunks fitted with a mattress, but he was held back by one of the *Altgefangene*.

"No, lad, those have to be earned. You start down there." He pointed to the far end of the barracks where the bunks had neither mattress nor blanket.

Another shiver ran down Johann's spine and he was grateful for his greatcoat – and the prospect of sharing some body heat with Helmut. It was April and while the days could be hot, the nights were still chilly.

Supper was a sorry affair, consisting of a ladleful of watery soup and a piece of black bread.

"What is this?" Helmut asked as he removed a wilted greenish leaf from his mouth.

"Stinging nettle," Karsten said. "Eat it; it's healthy for you."

Healthy? Johann frowned, but decided anything was better than nothing. And the plant might even contain some much-needed nutrients. Although he certainly would have preferred a hearty piece of meat.

At the thought of meat, his stomach forcefully clenched, protesting the empty promise. He hadn't eaten meat since the day he'd been captured months ago.

"What day is it today?" he asked, since he'd lost count during the long journey.

"Workday."

"Like every day."

"A good day to die."

He stared at the other prisoners, doubting their mental health. How long would it take him to lapse into an equally pathetic state of mind? He clenched his teeth, willing away the self-pity and desolation threatening to swallow him whole.

The night was cold and short, but an improvement over the cattle car. His first morning in the new camp started with wake-up call at four-thirty a.m. He rubbed his sore eyes and began to scratch his itching body.

"Bed bugs," Karsten said. "You never get used to them."

Oh, well. Another pleasantness to look forward to. Out of habit he'd slept in his clothes and jumped off the bunk bed, hungry as a wolf.

Unfortunately, there was no food. Only work. First, they had to stand in front of their bunks, waiting for the Russians to count them. The living and the dead were summed up and had to match the number on a list.

Thankfully, it did. Then the newcomers were ordered to remove the comrades who'd died during the night. Sixteen in total. Johann could only shake his head, but everyone else seemed to consider this a normal number for the barracks of three hundred prisoners.

"We've had fifty dead per night during winter," Karsten said. "Spring has really helped."

After that ghastly task was accomplished, Helmut grabbed Johann's elbow and led him to two of the bunks that were now empty. "They said we could use these. Do you want the top or the bottom?"

"Doesn't matter." Johann wanted to scream. His future looked bleak. His only hope was that the war would be over soon, and everyone would be released home. He could cling a few months to the thing they called *life*.

The men walked outside to a row of buckets stacked against the fence.

"What are we doing?" Johann asked.

"Getting water from the river." One of the old prisoners bent down and took a bucket in each hand. "Better get going, or there will be no breakfast."

His words frightened Johann's empty stomach and grabbing two buckets he followed the man in front of him to the exit.

"They let us leave the camp?" Gerd whispered, renewed hope in his voice.

Nobody bothered to answer. The column of prisoners walked in darkness to the river, accompanied by several armed guards. Johann eyed the flowing water with longing. It would be so nice to take a bath and rub off the layers of grime. But he didn't even reach near the river. The file stopped and his fellow prisoners started handing empty buckets down the line and full ones up, until everyone had two heavy buckets in their hands.

A whistle gave the sign to return and they trudged back to the camp. Carrying the heavy buckets cost Johann every bit of strength he had left, and he arrived at the camp out of breath, his arms sore and his back aching. He glanced into the empty eyes of the *Altgefangene* and observed their scuffling gait. They were but shells, devoid of an actual human being inside.

Every man was handed a tin cup full of water and the rest was used to make lunch, and dinner: a thin soup with stinging nettle. On a lucky day they'd find a morsel of potato at the bottom, but most of the days it was just soup.

Breakfast consisted of a piece of black bread. The bread was different than the one he knew from home. It was hard, but humid. The Russian word was *khleb*, but the German prisoners dubbed it *Klebe,* or glue, because it was slimy as soap and if you threw it against the wall it stuck there.

The bread stuck to the roof of the mouth, especially when eaten without water. But if chewed long enough, it became soft and sweet.

"A gift of God," Helmut, who'd been unusually quiet this morning, said.

Johann didn't have enough energy to engage in a conversation, so he simply nodded. Conserving what little energy he possessed had become his main concern. The breakfast took only five minutes and they lined up to hand over the dishes to the kitchen staff.

"If you want to survive, get a job in the kitchen," a man behind him murmured.

Johann looked up. The kitchen prisoner was by no means fat, but he didn't have the same zombie-like look as the rest of them. He wondered what one had to do to become kitchen staff or if it was simply a matter of the stars aligning.

Back in Brest-Litowsk the Russians had assembled the prisoners according to groups of professions, so he expected them to somehow make use of that information. But at yesterday's registrations nobody had asked for a profession. Every old prisoner attached himself to a work detail, while the newcomers were left to wait in the courtyard.

CHAPTER 5

A s the sun peeked over the horizon, haze covered the
fields. It gave the camp and its surroundings an eerie
appearance. In the waiting crowd Johann spotted Gerd and
walked over to him.

"Hello," Johann said. There wasn't much else to say. *Glad
you're alive. Is your barracks as horrible as ours? Did you sleep
well?*

"Hello," Gerd answered, peering at him with bloodshot
eyes. His face and neck were covered in red bites. Involuntarily, Johann touched his own neck, reminded of the
itching bug bites.

"Anyone know what's going to happen?" another
newcomer asked.

"No." The usually well-informed Gerd shook his head.
"As mute as maggots, those Ivans."

As if to contradict him, one of the guards yelled, "Line
up in single file."

Helmut gave a half-grin. "At least lining up is something we know how to do well."

A huge number of men neatly lined up in several long queues going from one end of the courtyard to the other one. They were left waiting for some time, until the next command was given.

"Strip naked."

Johann couldn't believe his ears and he hesitated a moment too long. A rifle butt thudded against his back, accompanied by a command he didn't understand.

Left and right his fellow prisoners took off their clothing and folded it neatly to lie in a pile by their feet. He swallowed and followed suit. It was embarrassing to stand in a row with several hundred naked men, with a few guards watching them closely and keeping their guns at hand.

But his embarrassment multiplied when about half an hour later a military vehicle sped through the gates and came to a halt a few feet away from the first row of prisoners. A female doctor climbed out of the passenger side and despite the cold air Johann felt the heat of shame climb up to his burning cheeks.

"It's a woman," Helmut whispered unnecessarily.

They hadn't set eyes on a woman in months and the first encounter had to be a doctor parading in front of them while they stood at attention completely naked. To add to his grievances she was not only female, but also young and even pretty.

He stared straight ahead, trying to forget his clothesless state, while the doctor walked down the file, inspecting each man. His distraction worked until she stood directly in front of him, her peachy face with the high cheekbones and the dark eyes looking directly at him.

"Name?"

"Johann Hauser." He cast his eyes to the ground and clenched his jaw, avoiding looking at her.

"Look up." She'd found his name on a list and put a mark beside it. Then she checked his eyes and ears. "Mouth open." She put her slender fingers inside and fingered the inside of his cheeks. He fought the overwhelming urge to bite down on her finger, so she'd go away.

Of course, this would only get him into trouble, so he stared ahead, pretending to be somewhere else. When her fingers finally left his mouth, he wanted to sag with relief, but the physical exam wasn't over yet.

After jotting down notes in Cyrillic letters on her list, she handed the clipboard to one of the guards and squeezed Johann's biceps hard. He almost let out a scream. When she seemed satisfied that she couldn't squeeze any harder, she said something in Russian and the guard scribbled letters on the list.

Another level of pure embarrassment hit him, when she ran her hands down his chest, abdomen, and thighs, squeezing those muscles the same way she had done with his biceps.

The guard by her side was busy recording whatever she told him. Johann didn't understand a single word. It didn't matter. The only thing he wanted was for her to move on to her next victim.

"Turn around," she said. Her German was good, with only a trace of the hard pronunciation native Russian speakers usually had.

To forget about his humiliation, Johann pondered where she'd learned German. Had she ever been in Germany? Maybe before the war? She seemed too young for that… a gasp escaped his throat when she grabbed both of his ass cheeks and pinched hard.

"Good." She seemed incredibly pleased. "Turn around. You're two."

Stupefied, he nodded, not sure what had occurred. Thankfully, she moved on to the next in line and once she was out of earshot, Johann whispered, "What was that about?"

"No idea," Helmut replied.

Gerd, though, had listened to the conversation between the doctor and the guards, and explained, "It seems this exam is some kind of classification. She measures the fat and muscle tissue and according to how much there is, we get put into one of four categories."

"Like cattle by weight?" If Johann could feel even more humiliated after enduring this examination, he would do so now.

"Kind of. I understood they use four numbers. One and two means suitable for hard labor. Three can do only light work. Four is too sick to work and will be taken to the hospital."

"I see." Johann wasn't sure whether he should be happy about being in such good shape.

The prisoners in the categories one and two were put into groups of fifty, seemingly at random. Gerd was in Johann's group, but Helmut got assigned to another one.

Johann felt a stab to his heart. Without his friend, he felt so... lonely. Such a notion reeked of absurdity, since he never had a moment truly on his own, not even when visiting the latrine. But as he followed the Romanian foreman to the exit of the camp, Johann couldn't whisk away the empty sadness filling his soul.

His detail trudged about two miles to their workplace: a dusty quarry. Johann wanted to weep when he saw the toiling comrades. With nothing but rusty shovels and poles they unearthed large stones and loaded them onto hand carts for other prisoners to haul to a construction site about one mile away.

Johann was assigned to a work unit loading up the rocks. It didn't take long until every muscle in his emaciated body protested from the backbreaking work. His hands raw and bleeding, he winced every time he hoisted up another rock.

After several hours of work, he barely managed to keep upright. Even the return walk from the cart to the quarry with empty hands was an ordeal. When he packed another rock, his feet refused to obey, and he sank to the ground. The Russian guards were quick to jump to his side and hit him furiously, shouting, *"Davai, davai."*

Even without Russian language skills Johan knew what it meant: *Quick, quick.* And he also knew what would happen if he didn't get up. He'd seen it many times before.

An image of Lotte appeared in his mind. She beckoned to

him not to give up and return to her. Her smile unearthed hidden energy reserves in him, and he somehow stumbled up, grabbed the damned rock with both hands and hauled it over to the cart. On the way back he would have wept, if he'd had a drop of liquid to spare inside his dry and dusty body.

The sun had reached her highest point and Johann wondered when they would get a break. Nothing happened. His growling stomach drowned out all other noises. It was bad enough to be hungry all the time when sitting idly in the camp or standing with cramping feet in a cattle car, but working like an ox?

He made another return trip to the handcart, when he saw Karsten coming from the other side of the quarry.

Johann acknowledged him with a tired nod. "How long until we get a break?"

"No break and no food until our shift ends at 3 p.m."

Johann almost fainted.

"You need to pace yourself." Karsten showed him how to work slowly enough to make it bearable, but steadily enough not to attract the ire of the guards. He also taught him the shuffling gait the *Altgefangene* had adopted to use the least amount of energy possible.

In the beginning it felt unnatural, almost as if time was slowing down. But much to his surprise, Karsten was right. The work was still excruciating, but the snail's pace made it bearable. The shuffling, empty-handed return walk gave his body a modicum of recovery to tackle the next round.

He also learned to take three additional steps and unload his burden on the shadow side of the cart, getting his head out of the scorching afternoon sun for a few minutes. It made a huge difference.

At three p.m., Johann was barely alive, swaying on his exhausted feet, but the day wasn't over yet. He clumped along with the rest of the tired men, two long miles until they reached the camp, where he flopped onto the ground, too weak to queue up for his share of soup. If it weren't for Helmut, who looked surprisingly fresh, Johann wouldn't have eaten that day.

"Here you go." Helmut handed him a bowl of soup. After looking at Johann's face, he added, "I won't ask how your day went."

Johann didn't answer, too busy downing his soup and the dark bread. He passed out immediately after eating, until someone shook his shoulder.

It was one of the Romanians, who served as helpers to the guards. "Get up, lazybones! Work needs to be done!"

Work? Johann blinked a few times; was it morning again? No, by the position of the sun, it must be early evening. Work details were assigned. Arriving food had to be carried from the gates to the kitchen, vegetables needed to be planted, and much more.

Johann was lucky. He was assigned to sweep the barracks, light work done inside, away from the prying eyes of the Romanian capos and out of the sun. He constantly eyed the bunks and yearned to just lie down and sleep. But he resisted, because he could vividly imagine what would happen if a capo found him asleep on duty. His sore back hurt enough without the addition of whip lashes or cosh punches.

When the housework was done, the prisoners finally had an hour of *leisure time*. Those on lighter work details had some energy left and gathered to read one of the few books that hadn't been confiscated yet. Or they simply sat and talked about home, their families, wives and sweethearts.

Helmut tried to persuade Johann to come with him to a Bible study group, but Johann shook his head. All he wanted was to sleep. He found his new bunk, which still carried the stench of its previous owner. But he didn't care. He wrapped himself into his greatcoat and fell into a death-like sleep, until the night was over at 4.30 a.m.

Wake-up call.

Another day like the one before, minus the humiliating examination.

And another one... week after week.

CHAPTER 6

One day, new information interrupted the boring routine.

"Germany has capitulated! The war is over!" the guards announced when Johann returned in the afternoon from his work detail.

They must have received the news hours ago, because the Russians, and most of the Romanians, were smashed. The smell of alcohol wafted across the camp and the guards could barely keep their rifles straight.

For a moment Johann thought about escape, but he understood the futility of such an attempt. Even if he managed to wrest away the rifle of one of the guards, the vast Russian grasslands were unforgiving. A man on foot would never make it past the thirty-five-mile cordon around the camp. Then he'd be picked up by soldiers and beaten to a pulp before he was brought back to die as a forbidding example for his fellow prisoners.

Since the guards were too inebriated to enforce the usual afternoon work, the prisoners settled in the courtyard. They talked – as usual – about the one thing foremost in their minds: going home. After all, the hope of seeing home again was what kept them alive despite all odds.

"We made it!" someone said.

"I never believed I'd survive the war." Gerd managed something resembling a smile.

"Everything will change now," Helmut said.

"It's surreal. I fear I'll wake up and find out I'm dreaming," Johann said.

"Want me to pinch you?"

"No, thanks." Johann remembered all too well the embarrassing pinches performed by the Russian doctor.

As the evening wore on, Gerd gathered his courage and asked one of the drunken Russians, "What will happen to us now that the war is over?"

The soldier laughed, as if it was the funniest joke he'd heard in years, slapped Gerd on the shoulders and said, "*Voina kaput. Vsye domoi.*"

"What did he say?" Johann asked.

"The war is over. Everyone goes home."

"That is good news, indeed." Johann's heart filled with jubilation. He couldn't wait to see Lotte again. She must be worried crazy about him, since he hadn't been allowed to send her a message about his whereabouts. Dreams of holding her in his arms again, getting married and starting their own family filled his heart.

That night he slept with a smile on his lips.

Home! Sweet Home!

～

The next day was business as usual. And the one after that…
two weeks later, the prisoners sent a delegation to the camp
administration to ask about the promised release.

"You will be released tomorrow."

But tomorrow never came.

Soon Johann hesitated to believe any of the promises the
Russians made. Better food, less work, blankets for the
night, return home… all of these things were promised on a
regular basis, but never manifested.

At least Johann was relieved from working in the quarry
and instead assigned to the lumber mill. Working there was
much less agonizing. Sometimes they had to haul trees from
the woods and he always offered to go, because he actually
enjoyed being in the woods.

Hauling felled trees to the lumber mill had several
advantages. First, the Russian guards were too lazy to
accompany them, knowing the prisoners couldn't escape
anyway. As long as they returned in time to feed the hungry
saws, nobody hurried them on with screams and punches.
But the far more important advantage was the opportunity
to organize food. The prisoners would scavenge for edible
plants and berries to supplement their meager diet.

One day, a comrade saw a hare with two kittens. Johann
reacted instinctively and threw a stone at the smallest one.

"Good shot," his fellow said with admiration. Together
they walked to pick up the wounded animal. Johann broke
its neck and hid it under his shirt. The poor animal would
provide a nice meal for him and his closest friends tonight.

The rabbit's soft fur was smooth against his belly and he wished he'd had fur mittens last winter. He didn't think he'd still be here next winter, but if he used the fur to make mittens, he could barter them for food.

As summer broke the food rations increased slightly. Still not enough to calm the raging hunger Johann felt every minute of every day, but at least he stopped losing weight.

Thanks to the vegetables they had planted at the camp, every prisoner received one onion and one tomato per week, a much-needed delight among the otherwise drab meals.

"I can't believe it," Johann said, savoring the almost ripe tomato the size of a tennis ball.

"It's a gift from heaven." Helmut closed his eyes and sighed. He'd become awfully haggard, and Johann suspected he didn't look much better himself.

"I remember having toiled like a mule for this gift."

"God gives to those who don't sit idle."

"Do you have an answer to everything?" Johann asked and answered the question himself. "Yes, you do. I have no idea how you can still believe in a just God, when he lets us rot in this hellhole."

"His ways are mysterious. But if I didn't believe that all my suffering held a bigger meaning, I wouldn't have the strength to get up in the morning." Helmut's eyes opened and Johann glimpsed a rare flash of total desperation in them.

"I had no idea…" he murmured. He'd always mocked his friend for his unshakable belief, but he'd never considered it was the one pillar that kept Helmut alive.

In contrast to himself, Helmut didn't have a girl waiting

for him to return. Lotte served as Johann's anchor, and the dream of returning to her was his reason to survive just another day. Without that goal, he'd have given up already and turned crazy, running into the forbidden area near the fence around the camp.

Every other day a man who couldn't take the abuse any longer did just that, in the hopes the guards would shoot him dead. It was the one promise the Russians always made good on. Nobody had to wait long for the redeeming bullet.

Lying in the sun, nibbling at his raw onion, Johann put the cruel winter behind, intending never to think of it again. "What do you think? Will they let us go home before winter returns?"

"I sure hope so," Gerd said.

"Have you heard? There'll be a transport home soon," Jens, a short, sickly former tank driver said.

"*Skoro domoi!*" Helmut scoffed. "If they say, 'home soon' one more time, I'll vomit on their feet."

Johann opened his eyes in shock, the outburst completely out of character for his friend. "Are you alright?"

"Never been better."

A short silence ensued, until Karsten broke the silence. "Don't believe the rumors until they come with a list."

Johann had come to like the quiet man who kept a strict but just regimen in their barracks. And he'd always be indebted to him for the tips during his first days as slave laborer in the quarry.

"A list?" Gerd laughed.

"Yes. A list. The Russians put anything and everything on a list. Do you really believe they'd send us home without making and remaking endless lists first?" Karsten asked.

"You're probably right." Johann scratched the stubble on his head. For hygienic reasons the common prisoners had to shear their heads every two weeks. A few longhairs had achieved the privileged status of maintaining their hair by providing sought-after skills to the Soviet officers.

CHAPTER 7

Voronezh, September 1945

B y the end of summer rumors of release ran wild once again, when an official Soviet delegation arrived to inspect the camp. The party official from Moscow held a lengthy speech about the benefits and advantages of communism and closed with the words, *"Skoro domoi!"* Home soon.

Karsten's warning lingering in his mind, Johann held his hopes in check. But the next day another delegation arrived, consisting of three doctors. All prisoners, even the sick ones, were ordered into the courtyard.

Helmut groaned. "Not a physical examination again."

Johann had gotten used to the monthly examination. The prisoners even joked about what they called *Arschkneifen*, pinching your ass. It seemed to be the state-of-the-art method by which the Russian doctors determined whether a man was able to work or not.

The chief doctor explained that the weakest prisoners would be sent home first, with the others following after a short time. Johann felt dizzy. For the first time since being captured, hope sparked to life in his soul.

"They're making a list. They're really sending us home," he whispered.

Helmut nodded. "Let's hope we're weak enough."

Johann glanced at Helmut; whose condition had deteriorated considerably over the past month. He'd caught a nasty infection and had been excused from work for the past two weeks. Then his gaze wandered to the man in front of him. Karsten.

He hadn't seen Karsten since he'd been transferred to the camp hospital. The emaciated man swayed more than he stood, covered from head to toe in red blisters oozing pus.

Helmut followed Johann's glance and murmured, "He'll be on the list for sure."

"Did you know that he recently completed his fourth year in captivity?"

"Poor man. He really deserves to go home."

"We all do." Johann doubted that God had some kind of master plan, but if He did, Johann was sure he'd paid his dues for past sins more than once already. He'd never been intentionally cruel, had avoided participating in the killing of civilians and had basically done what every soldier did: fight for his country and obey orders.

This woman in China, the Jewess who'd helped him, she had sowed a seed of doubt in his heart. And with every atrocity committed in this war, Johann couldn't help but remember her and wonder about Hitler's words. Was the Jewish race really the root of all evil? Should they all be exterminated?

Deep down in his heart, Johann had known all along that it was wrong to condemn an entire race, but he'd let stubbornness and fear keep him from acting. Was the horrible captivity his punishment for being a coward?

Helmut and Karsten made it onto the "Homegoer List," but Johann didn't. With his newfound hope shattered into a million pieces, for days he moped around, refusing to speak a single word. At first, Helmut tried to cheer him up, but Johann couldn't stand to look at his best friend.

You're going home and leaving me here. To die alone.

The one person who'd been his pillar in this bleak world would now leave. He didn't begrudge Helmut the opportunity to return home, because how could he? But he hated the thought of being left behind. And he hated the pitying look in Helmut's eyes. Pity mixed with a sense of guilt.

"We'll get on the next transport, for sure." Gerd sidled up to Johann on the walk from the lumber mill to the camp.

"If you say so…" Johann didn't wish to discuss his shattered hopes with anyone, not even with a commiserating soul. For a short few hours, he had basked in the glow of hope. But the announcement of the results of the medical examination had been like a hammer blow to his spirit.

Three days passed and he still felt like hovering outside his mistreated body. He would cry if he had liquid to spare.

Or scream if he had energy. But he only toiled and trudged, breathed and slept, ate and drank, unable to fight his way back into life.

"You can't give up now," Gerd insisted. "We've survived so much. Just hold on a little bit longer."

"How much longer?" Johann stared at the man with empty eyes.

"It won't be long. Once the first transport is gone…"

"It's been three days and they're still here. What if it's another ruse to keep up our morale?"

Gerd's eyes flashed with fear, but only for a moment. "If it is, it sure didn't help to boost your morale." Then he slowed his step, falling behind.

Johann felt remorse over his snide comment but welcomed the silence. If only everyone would leave him alone. He was done with this life.

Several weeks passed and nothing happened. The *Heimkehrer*, the homegoers, lived in a constant maelstrom of conflicting emotions, hope quickly washed away by anguish. Joy faded into sadness. Out of two hundred men destined for the transport fifteen died in the first week. New lists were made, successors chosen.

Other men improved in health – and were kicked off the list, Helmut being one of them.

October passed, then November and still nobody had left the camp. Johann's state of mind didn't improve. He didn't bemoan his fate anymore but had fallen into a dull resignation. Nothing and no one were capable of making him *feel*. He slurped his soup in the same resigned way he shuffled his feet. There truly wasn't a spirit left inside the shell of his body.

He had stopped caring and might as well be dead already. Not even the floggings from the guards could tear him out of his nothingness. The dwindling daylight as fall approached pushed him even deeper into depression.

One day shortly after the arrival of the New Year, Karsten approached him, looking clean and tidy in new clothes. "Hey, I came to say goodbye."

"Bye." Johann looked the other way.

"They allowed us a bath, poured that disgusting delousing powder over us and even gave us new clothes."

"Good for you." Johann wanted to walk away, but Karsten put a hand on his arm.

"Don't make it harder than it is. This is only the beginning and soon you'll all be on your way home."

"If I live long enough…"

Karsten grinned. "I survived this hellish camp and the half dozen others before for more than four years. And so will you. But that's not the reason I came. Your girl's from Berlin, right?"

"Yes." A spark ignited in Johann's chest. Since the day of the list announcement he had pushed away thoughts of Lotte, because it was too painful to think of her. But now he couldn't keep burying his head in the sand, and the image of her sweet face returned with a vengeance.

He knew exactly what she'd say to him. *You're a pathetic weakling! You're willing to give up your life and me, simply because you weren't amongst the two hundred sickest men of the camp? It's about time you stopped moping around and fought back. I'm waiting for you and you'd better do everything in your power to return to my side!*

"Did you hear me?"

Johann blinked, Lotte's sweet voice fading away to be replaced by Karsten's.

"Did you even hear what I said?" Karsten asked again.

"Sorry, no."

"I said I can take a letter for you."

"A letter?" Johann's brain worked excruciatingly slowly these days. "Letters are forbidden." The Soviets were paranoid about the written word and the entire camp, including the prisoners, were searched on a regular basis for hidden diaries. Getting paper and pen was next to impossible, but some men still managed to do so and found joy and sanity in writing down their experiences.

Over the course of the past year, the other men had started relaying their own cruel, sad, funny, or simply mundane anecdotes to the committed writers. It was a desperate effort to be remembered, to let the world know about the horrible things they had to endure.

"So is organizing food," Karsten said with a grin.

"Right. But dying at work is forbidden, too, and men still do it."

"See?" Karsten handed him a tiny smudged piece of thick paper that had been a flour sack in its previous life and a pen.

"Thanks. When are you leaving?"

Karsten scoffed. "Soon... or so the Soviets say."

Even Johann had to smile. *Skoro* was one of the words most used by the officials, along with *kaput*. While *skoro* translated to soon, it could mean any time span between now and never. "Well, then, I should hurry up. See you at bedtime."

"See you."

Johann poured all his love into the letter for Lotte. Due to having only a tiny scrap of paper at his disposal, he designed the letter first in his head, before he committed it to paper.

Beloved Darling,

I hope this letter finds you well. They are releasing the first prisoners and I hope to follow soon. Rest assured that my love for you grows stronger every day. The promise of holding you in my arms once again is what keeps me fighting to survive.

Forever yours,

Johann

The simple act of getting his thoughts together and writing the letter somehow infused him with the strength to overcome his depression and have a more positive outlook on the future again. His captivity wouldn't last forever. He just had to hold on a bit longer. And then he could restart his life with Lotte by his side.

A life devoid of war, fighting, bombs, hunger, pain, thirst, cold, beatings, bug bites, sores, distrust, fear, sickness, slave labor, raw hands, nostalgia, and misery. In short, a life worth living.

He rummaged in his pockets and found what he'd been looking for: a soft piece of wood he'd worked on for endless hours with a spoon, making it resemble a doll. In the evening he sought Karsten. The sick man had been released from the hospital but had not been declared fit to work.

"Thanks so much for doing this. Here's my letter and a gift for my girl. How will you send it?"

"I'll find out when I'm in Germany. I still don't believe they'll really let me go after such a long time."

"Our country has changed," Johann said and squinted at the man who'd become a good friend. "When was the last time you visited?"

"August 1940."

Johann paused for a moment. Back then, before the constant air raids, Germany had been beautiful. "It's nothing like that anymore. When I was on furlough the last time, Munich was a heap of rubble. And it was considered one of the least badly destroyed cities."

Karsten swallowed. "My wife was pregnant when I left. I don't even know…" Tears sprang to his eyes and he couldn't finish the sentence. The prisoners avoided the expression of emotions at all costs, because sadness was contagious. Johann swiveled his head, pretending he'd heard something.

Meanwhile, Karsten regained his composure and said in an offhand remark, "You guys will need to fabricate lamps for winter."

"I know." Johann was glad the conversation had reached steady ground again. "Heinrich has already tasked us with organizing tin cans."

"He's a good one. Quite the ingenious engineer." It was true; Heinrich could repair anything under the sun and used the most mundane spare parts to build small wonders of technology.

As more and more men returned to the barracks, getting ready for the night, Johann impressed Lotte's address and her official name upon Karsten. "Don't forget it, will you?"

"I won't. I promise to deliver this letter dead or alive." Karsten chuckled and patted the precious cargo.

"What if they confiscate it?" A shiver snaked up Johann's spine.

"In that case, I'll personally deliver the message. I'll tell her that you're very much in love and keeping your chin up."

"Thank you again. I wish you good luck. Greet Germany for me!"

CHAPTER 8

Berlin, February 1946

Thinking of Johann every single day, Lotte worried about his fate. Rumors about the deplorable treatment of German prisoners of war by the Russians abounded, but Lotte refused to dwell on them, hoping they were just that: rumors.

One day after work she was lying on the sofa listening to a radio program when a knock sounded at the apartment door. She was the only person in the apartment, since the rest of the family had gone out to run errands.

With a deep sigh she got up and dragged her tired bones to the door, already formulating a snide remark for whoever had forgotten his or her keys and disturbed her well-earned rest. Even after her body had adjusted to the backbreaking work as a *Trümmerfrau*, one of the women clearing the rubble from Berlin, she returned home every evening with aching bones and raw hands.

"What…?" She peered at the most haggard, ill-looking man she'd ever seen. There was barely a hair on his head and every inch of exposed skin was covered in red dots, some of them oozing pus.

His hollow eyes focused on her with some difficulty and he said, "I'm looking for Alexandra Wagner."

The words were a punch to her stomach, and she gasped for breath. Nobody she knew used her fake name anymore. "Who are you?"

"A comrade of Johann."

Her heart melted and she gave the man a once-over. It wasn't the wisest thing to do, inviting a bedraggled stranger into her home when she was alone. But despite his dreadful appearance, she was certain he wouldn't pose a threat to her.

"I'm Alexandra. Would you like to come inside?" she asked, only to wish she hadn't as an appalling stench wafted into her nostrils when he agreed. Forcing down the vomit coming up her throat she led him into the kitchen.

"Please have a seat. Do you want a glass of water?" He greedily nodded and she added, "And something to eat?"

"That would be grand." His smile bared a row of black and broken teeth.

Lotte turned her head away at the foul stench leaving his mouth and filled a glass with water, before she rummaged through the pantry to find a piece of bread and some cheese.

"Here you go." She sat across the table, a safe distance

from him, trying not to stare at the oozing dots on his face, neck and hands.

"Thank you." He emptied the glass of water and then began talking. "I'm Karsten. Your fiancé Leutnant Johann Hauser and I were together in a Russian POW camp in Voronezh."

Lotte hissed and thousands of questions attacked her, but she didn't interrupt his laborious speech, which was only interrupted by careful chewing of the bread she'd given him.

"They let me go, because," he scoffed and gestured to his body, "as you can see, I'm of no use to them anymore. I'm too sick to work. Johann gave me a letter for you, but it was confiscated by the bloody Soviets before I crossed the border. So I can only give you this." He took a tiny piece of wood from his pocket. "He made this for you, so you have something to remember him by."

A wave of emotions washed over her, and she had to will away the tears forming in her eyes as she took the wood and looked at it. It had the form of a body and traces of a face, and with much imagination she recognized it was indeed a doll resembling Johann.

"Thank you," she said, her voice trembling. "Is he... well?"

"*Well* is a word I wouldn't use to describe any of my comrades, but he's alive and in a much better condition than I am. Although it was only my deplorable condition that caused them to send me home." He stared at her. "You are exactly like he described. Beautiful. He said to let you know he loves you very much and only the thought of returning to you makes him stay strong day after day."

Tears ran unchecked down Lotte's cheeks and she squeezed the wooden doll in her hand. "Thank you so much for going to the trouble to come here and find me. You can't imagine how much this news means to me."

"Anything for a dear comrade like Johann. I hope he and the others will return soon."

"Can I do something else for you?"

"No, thanks. I need to catch my train to Oldenburg and see if I can find my family," he said, rising.

"God bless you." Lotte cut another piece of bread, fully aware that she'd go without dinner tonight if she gave it to him. "Here, take this for the journey. I'm sorry, but I don't have more."

"That is a lot, actually." He bared his rotten teeth again in something that might have resembled a smile in another time and place and then left the apartment.

"Who was that man?" Her sister Ursula entered the apartment with a concerned look on her face that shifted into full-blown panic when she saw the traces of tears on her sister's face. "What did he do to you?"

"Nothing," Lotte bawled, holding out her hand with the wooden doll. "He's… a… friend of Johann."

"That's good news, isn't it?" Ursula's question came out hesitantly.

"I guess. This man, he was a prisoner in the same camp with Johann."

"That means Johann is still alive, and that is a good thing." Ursula sat on the sofa beside Lotte and put an arm around her shoulders.

"The Russians confiscated the letter Johann sent me.

Why would they even do this?" Lotte wiped the tears from her face.

"I don't know. Maybe he wrote something the censors didn't like?"

Another round of sobs shook Lotte's body. "So we're back to having censors again? Wasn't that supposed to end with the Nazi reign?"

"It was, but since Johann is still a prisoner, I guess they still censor the letters."

Lotte looked at her sister, not knowing whether she should be happy or sad. Her darling was still alive, but after she'd seen Karsten's deplorable state she wasn't sure that was a good thing. Another thought tormented her mind and she blurted out, "I don't even know where Voronezh is!"

"Me neither." Ursula glanced around the living room. "If Richard was here, we could ask him." Their brother had spent most of his leisure time with his nose stuck in a book – any book – during their youth.

"Or look it up in his school atlas." Lotte felt a surge of energy. "I'll go to the public library tomorrow and find out where Voronezh is. And now I'll write a letter to Johann." She got up, leaving a perplexed Ursula on the sofa.

She sat down and wrote,

My dearest Johann,

You can't imagine my utter joy when your friend Karsten appeared on our doorstep today and brought news about you. He said you were well and alive, but I still worry about you. If this letter reaches you, please let me know if there's anything you need. If they let me send you a package, I'll certainly do so.

As for me, I'm fine. I arrived in Berlin last summer after an adventurous evacuation from Norway. Are you up to date with the news? Berlin has been divided into four sectors, one for each of the victorious powers.

The city is completely in ruins; it's a miracle that our building is still standing. I took on work as a Trümmerfrau, removing the debris to build new things. It's a tough job, but I won't complain. I'm fine.

She rubbed her aching back; unsure what else she should tell him. She didn't want to sound negative, didn't want to complain about hunger, cold and the miserable living conditions in Berlin. The way Karsten had looked, conditions in Russia must be much more deplorable than she could even imagine.

My father is still not home, but Anna, Ursula, Richard, and Mutter, they all survived the war. I shall hope that you will meet them very soon.

You remember, Gerlinde, my friend from Warsaw? She stayed in Hamburg looking for her own family.

Now that she thought about it, she regretted that she hadn't asked Karsten about Johann's parents. Would he give them the message, too? Or should she do this? She'd never met them, but Johann had given her their address in Munich. Yes, she'd write a letter to them, too. His mother must be worried sick about her only son.

I'm going to give your parents the happy news that you are alive, and once I hear back from them, I'll let you know.

My beloved darling, I think of you every waking minute and dream of you every night. My biggest wish is for you to return soon and hold me in your arms.

Love forever,
Lotte

. . .

She put a kiss on the paper and traced the barely visible mark with her pen. Then she assessed her work and drew a heart next to it. She folded the letter and put it into an envelope, addressing it to Leutnant Johann Hauser, POW Camp, Voronezh, Russia

The next day before work, she went to the Red Cross office to send the letter. The friendly woman at the reception couldn't promise the letter would reach its recipient, because they'd had some difficulties getting the Russian authorities to actually distribute the stacks of mail sent via the Red Cross. But she encouraged Lotte to return every month with a new letter, because a letter not sent never had a chance to be delivered.

CHAPTER 9

Winter returned with all its might and every evening after work the men busied themselves making their barracks cozy. Under Heinrich's guidance they organized old tin cans, bottles, and petrol, hiding the booty in secret holes beneath the hut.

"I really miss Karsten," Johann said, cutting super-thin strips from a blanket with a wooden knife. Each time he had three strips, about ten inches long, he handed them to Helmut.

"He'll be home by now and we will be soon, too." Helmut had taken the disappointment of being swept off the *Heimkehrer* list surprisingly well. As always, he found solace in the Bible. His positive mindset was contagious, and Johann looked slightly more optimistically into the future.

Helmut took the threads and twirled them into a cord, which he handed down to the next man in line.

"No, not like that." Heinrich scrutinized the wick and

returned it to Helmut. "It has to be twirled tighter, or it won't work."

As soon as Helmut was done, he showed his work to Heinrich again, who gave an appreciative nod and tied a knot at both ends. The next man in line was tasked with soaking the cord in the liquid petrol they'd pilfered from the camps' vehicles.

Heinrich examined the work again, gave a few hints here and there, and took the soaked wicks to let them dry. Meanwhile other men prepared the container, using either a tin can or a bottle to make the lamp. Bottles were preferred because they gave more light, but they were also harder to organize.

Johann looked at the row of wicks hanging to dry. Having light in the barracks during the long winter months was something to look forward to. At the lumber mill they had collected small wood remnants and a group of fellow prisoners drilled holes into them.

It was ridiculous, but his heart was pounding with suspense. Would it work? Forcing the slight tremble from his hands, he took one of the dried wicks, removed the knot and threaded it through the piece of wood. Then he handed it to Heinrich. "It was your idea. You light the first one."

Heinrich's eyes gleamed with joy as he poured some of the pilfered petrol into a tin can and dropped the wood with the wick inside. Then he lit a match.

All two hundred men in the barracks held their breath as Heinrich's hand hovered over the can. An explosive flame shot up, but settled into a steady flicker after a few moments.

"It works! We have light!" someone screamed with joy.

Quickly they manufactured more lamps and distributed them across the hut. Heinrich gave strict orders not to waste petrol and only to light them for an hour or two each evening before bedtime.

The lamps smoldered like chimneys, spitting black clouds into the already thick air, but that didn't spoil the happiness of the men.

One day the Soviets sent another delegation to the camp and instituted educational classes for the prisoners to teach them the many advantages of communism. Attendance was obligatory.

"What exactly are we doing here?" Johann whispered.

"Listening to what the Soviets have to say," Gerd answered.

Johann cast him a dark stare. In his opinion, this was lost time that could be better spent on mending his torn tunic. The door to the big room in the administrative building opened, and the men went inside. A fire burned in a crate and warmed the room.

"They've gone all out to show us how well they're doing," Helmut remarked.

"I'll take the warmth. But I won't convert to another fascist ideology."

"Shush."

Johann furtively glanced around, but nobody was within earshot. Although one could never be entirely sure about the Russian bastards and their helpers. The sadistic Romanians had been sent home in the fall, along with the

Yugoslavs and others from the new *brother nations*. Former SS men and those who had no qualms over betraying their own kind had taken their place. The position came with perks: more food, less work, better treatment.

The Soviet official held a lengthy speech about Marx, Engels, Lenin and, naturally, Stalin. He ended his sermon with the words, "We're here to end the evil of fascism and are offering you the opportunity to become better people. Therefore you're invited to join the Antifascist Committee that has been installed in this camp. You can sign your membership on the forms near the door. Any questions?"

Nobody dared ask.

The officer made a satisfied face and said, "Who wants to be the first one?"

Some men rushed to the door and, under celebratory shouts of the guards, were welcomed as anti-fascists and members of the brotherly communist society.

Johann glanced around. The majority of the prisoners didn't seem willing to defect and join the ranks of the former enemy.

Since not enough men had jumped at the generous opportunity, the Soviet officer, who surely had a quota to fill, clapped his hands and said, "Everyone who refuses to renounce his abominable fascist ideas and doesn't voluntarily join the Antifascist Committee will be treated as the traitor he is."

Immediately a big number of prisoners rushed to fill the forms.

"Do we have to sign right now?" someone asked.

"No, no. Of course not. This is completely voluntary,

and you can take as much time for consideration as you wish."

"I'm never going to sign," Johann murmured under his breath as they returned to their barracks.

Helmut cast him a surprised glance. "Why would you say that? Haven't you told me many times what Hitler did was wrong?"

"It was. But what Stalin does is equally wrong. I'm not committing the same mistake twice."

About half of the men had joined the ranks of the communists, and surprisingly, the rest of the men were left alone. The officer had reached his quota and that was what mattered. Antifascists had slightly better conditions, but Johann decided it wasn't enough to justify betraying his own conscience.

As the cruel winter wore on men were dying like flies left and right. The unbearable cold and ever-dwindling rations, combined with arduous work, was too much to bear. They passed out at work, never to stand up again, froze to death in their sleep, succumbed to infectious diseases or simply closed their eyes when the last morsel of life energy in their broken bodies had been used up.

One day Helmut relayed the rumor of another transport for home leaving soon.

Johann pulled a face. "And you still believe this? Haven't you heard the Russian saying, 'Please forgive me for not promising anything today'?"

Gerd nodded. "Never heard more fitting words. Empty promises are all they've given us so far."

"I'm starting to think they do this on purpose. Dangle

the possibility of freedom in front of us, get our hopes up to keep our behavior in check."

"Why would they even bother?"

"To extract more work from us," Helmut said. "A man without hope has no reason to work. We all do everything to stay alive for the sole reason that we want to go home."

"That's kind of depressing. To know they can blackmail us to work for them with the dream of seeing our families again, even if they have no intention of ever making good on that promise," Heinrich said.

Like the three of them, Heinrich hadn't joined the Antifascists. They had discussed the topic again and again and always decided a bit of bread wasn't worth selling one's soul.

But today, as the hunger gnawed more viciously than ever, Gerd suddenly said, "It's not reprehensible wanting to live, right?"

Johann peered at him, sensing the change in conviction. "No, it's not."

"Right. I can't take it anymore. I'm gonna join those bastards. Just yesterday Rolf told me that you get an entire loaf of bread for your signature."

"You do what you must." Johann looked at Gerd, hoping this wouldn't be the end of their friendship.

CHAPTER 10

The horrific winter passed, and Johann and Helmut remained alive. How, they did not know. Working every day, all day, with next to no food, despicable sanitary conditions and the ever-present cold.

The spring sunshine warmed the air and melted away the snow. For a short time Johann cursed the thick mud they had to wade through every day. But now, his own life looked less bleak due to the splendid weather.

Throughout winter, Gerd had taught them the basics of Russian, and Johann was able to understand most of the commands and even hold a very basic conversation.

New prisoners arrived from some other camp and Johann climbed the hierarchy ladder to become a *resident prisoner*, with a slightly better standing compared to the newcomers. He jumped at the opportunity when a nearby *kolkhoz*, a collective farm, asked for workers.

The farmer in charge of that particular piece of land was an old, sturdy man. His bushy eyebrows and a long, grey beard gave him a grim look. He examined the *plenni*, the German prisoners, carefully and shook his head, muttering, "Too thin to work."

Then he talked in rapid-fire Russian with the guard and Johann could only guess at his words. The guard shook his head, and Johann believed he understood, "No. These are the strongest ones we have."

Well, *strong* wasn't the word Johann would use to describe anyone in the camp. Skin, bones, and sinew were all they possessed. Every last ounce of fat and muscle had been used up by their starved bodies to keep the heart pumping and the lungs breathing.

The farmer, Igor Smirnov, shrugged and addressed the *plenni* in a short speech – translated by the guard – outlining the tasks and threatening severe punishment should they fail to work hard and honestly.

Johann was used to hard work and vicious beatings should he be too slow for the guards' liking. This was nothing new and didn't scare him. As long as the blows didn't crack his skin, he could handle it. Open wounds, though, were a different matter to deal with. So, he suspiciously eyed the pitchfork in the farmer's hand. It would mean sure death to be speared by that dirty thing.

The first task was to plant potatoes – tedious work in the heavy, loamy earth. After a short time Johann's back throbbed and ached from maintaining a bent-over position and he cursed having signed up for this labor detail.

So far it hadn't proven advantageous compared to the known grind at the lumber mill. But then, much to his surprise – and the disdain of the guards – Smirnov's wife came to the field with a huge pot.

Lunch? During work hours? This was something Johann hadn't experienced since being taken captive. The guards and the woman exchanged a few sharp words, but she only shook her head and put the pot down, distributing spoons to the *plenni*.

Johann hesitated to stop working, afraid of the guards' retaliation, but he couldn't resist the encouraging nod of the old woman for long. A few seconds later he dropped his shovel and stormed with his fellow prisoners toward the food.

A dozen hungry men dipped their spoons simultaneously into the big pot of watery soup. It was by no means a hearty meal, but it was something to fill the growling stomach. And a short reprieve from the backbreaking work.

All too soon, the barrage of spoons scraped the pot empty and the guards hurried them back to planting potatoes. There was a quota to fill and work to be done. Johann was deliciously rested, and his stomach stopped growling, busy with digesting the unexpected food.

Farmer Smirnov came to scrutinize their work in the afternoon and, judging by the glint in his eyes, he was pleased with the progress the prisoners had made. He and the guard talked for a while and Johann gleaned from the exchange that they were ahead of schedule to meet the target.

"We should slow down," he whispered to his neighbor, one of the new arrivals.

"Why? If we hurry up, we can finish early."

Johann scoffed. "In your dreams. They'll only put us to other work and raise the target for tomorrow."

Another man, called Reiner, chimed in. "Johann's right.

Never give the Russians more than they ask for. The goal is a sacred cow and has to be reached at all costs. Exceeding the target should only be done with careful measure, and only if there's a reward to it."

The newcomer stared at them. "But that's so stupid!"

"Welcome to communism as it really is," Johann said.

The next day, Johann and Reiner were tasked with mucking out the pigsty. Sweat was running down his forehead in rivulets as he carried the loaded fork to the dung heap. After half a morning's work, he undertook the trip to the dung heap for the last time and paused a few moments to take a leak into the muck.

When he returned to the pigsty, Reiner was crouched over the feeding trough, greedily shoving the scraps meant for the pigs into his mouth. Momentarily stunned, Johann stopped in his tracks, mouth hanging agape. What this fellow was doing was strictly forbidden. Stealing food, even if only from the pigs, was punished with a heavy beating, penal work and a day in solitary detention – without food or water.

But glancing at the potato peels, half-rotten carrots and wilting lettuce, he couldn't resist the allure. Glancing over his shoulder to make sure nobody lurked nearby, he launched himself at the trough, shoving food into his mouth.

Oblivious to anything but the grinding of his teeth, Johann didn't notice the big man approaching the pigsty. Only when the frame filled the door and cast a shadow in the sty did he turn around and wait with trepidation for the inevitable punishment.

Farmer Smirnov stood in the door, looking at the two

plenni rummaging in the pigswill. His jaw dropped, aghast at the spectacle in front of his eyes.

"*Tovarish*, please..." Johann uttered.

The farmer glowered at him, the vein in his neck pulsating dangerously, but then he turned around and walked away.

"He let us off the hook," Johann hissed, heaving like a locomotive.

Reiner flopped to the ground, the slop drooling from his lips. "He could be back with the guard. We'd better..."

"Better what?" There was nothing they could do. If Smirnov reported them, they were done for. Nobody would even ask a German prisoner whether the accusation was true or not.

"We'd better finish our last meal and die with a full stomach," Reiner said, scavenging for the last scraps of edibles. Johann followed suit, both of them shivering with fear.

But nothing happened. Smirnov didn't return, and neither did the guard. They cleaned up and walked over to the potato field to continue working with their comrades. Just before it was time to return to the camp, the farmer and his wife showed up on the field, handing a bottle of clear water to the *plenni*. The bottle made its round, and Johann took a measured gulp. Barely enough to quench his maddening thirst, but a welcome refreshment for the long way home.

He handed the bottle back to Smirnov, who didn't flinch. Yet Johann believed he'd seen him wink. In the evening, Johann divided his bread into three parts and gave one each to Gerd and Helmut.

"Why so generous?" Helmut asked.

There were too many men around and one could never be sure who was a spy, ratting out a comrade for an extra meal, so he simply said, "I'm not hungry."

Helmut gave him a disbelieving stare, but Gerd took the bread without a qualm. Chewing, he said, "I've been hungry only once since the bastards captured me. Perpetually."

It was an old joke, but Johann chuckled. Today, he ironically felt almost like a human being again, happy, and sated with pigswill.

He worked on the farm for several weeks, and Smirnov always looked away when the prisoners devoured food that wasn't meant for them. The pigs didn't seem to mind either.

One evening, a group of prisoners was lying on the grass outside the barracks, enjoying a moment of rest and thinking of home.

"When do you think they're going to let us go?" Reiner asked.

"Who knows?" Gerd scratched the mosquito bites on his arms. These little insects were even more annoying than the bed bugs, sucking on the blood of the weakened men.

Johann gazed at the light blue sky above him. Pink and orange hues were creeping up the horizon as the sun went down in the west. Soon, the entire sky would burn in the brightest orange and red like a flaring fire.

It irked him. More than a year had passed since the end of World War II and the Russians showed no intention of releasing their prisoners. Who the hell did these bastards think they were? And what gave them the right to keep him and his comrades prisoners… and for how long? Would he have to struggle through another cruel winter? Could he?

Despite the slightly better conditions on the farm, Johann doubted that he had the stamina to withstand another winter in the camp. The anger of so many months boiled in his intestines and suddenly broke free.

"Those damn Russians! Anti-fascism my ass! Communism is worse than Nazism ever was. Worship the sacred cows of Stalin, the Party and the five-year plan, whether it makes any sense or not. Sooner or later they'll ruin their people and their country with this stupidity."

Helmut looked at him with shell-shocked eyes. "Shush. If they hear you…"

"Let them hear me, fascist swine!" The words tumbled out of Johann's mouth. When his brain caught up, his mouth hung agape and he glanced around, frightened, at the men present. Gerd and Helmut wouldn't report him, he was sure of that. Neither would Reiner, his partner in crime from the pigsty. But there were two or three other men whose allegiances he couldn't quite place. Well, it was too late and there was nothing he could do but wait.

He didn't have to wait for long. The next day, after work, he was called to the camp administration. After a short interrogation, he was informed that as of the following day, he was relieved of his duties at the farm and assigned to the coal mine.

Johann remembered well his months working in the quarry at the beginning of his imprisonment in this camp, and he involuntarily shivered. The coal mine was said to be worse.

A glint of triumph filled the commandant's eyes as he said, "This will teach you to appreciate the goodwill of the Russian people."

Goodwill of the Russian people. Johann fought the urge to retch on the official's shoes. Apart from the Smirnov couple, no other person had showed him goodwill in all these months. But he knew better than to dissent, and kept his eyes glued to the floor. A loose mouth had brought him here and he had no desire to worsen an already ugly situation.

"Yes, *gospodin* commandant," he said and waited for the officer to dismiss him.

Once outside, Helmut waited for him anxiously. "And?"

"The coal mine."

"Damn." Helmut's eyes filled with shock. "But it could have been worse."

"It could." Johann tried to put a good face on the matter. They might have given him a detention, food deprivation, a beating, or any kind of additional punishment. "I guess I should consider myself lucky?"

"Let's agree that you should keep your mouth shut more often." Helmut gave him a crooked grin. Helmut had a comparatively easy job as locksmith, because the Russians valued his expertise and ingenuity. He'd tried several times to get Johann assigned to his work detail, but it had never worked.

Johann knew his friend was worried about him. The coal mine had the highest mortality rate of all labor details. Every day, several of the men didn't return to the camp in the evening. In summer, that is, because in winter even more perished. The inevitable replenishment of the coal mine detail was one of the most feared occasions in the camp.

"Does that mean I won't get part of your rations

anymore?" Helmut made such a puppy-eyed face that Johann had to laugh against his will.

"I guess you're actually the unlucky guy here."

"I guess I am. Mostly because I'll have to put up with your moaning and groaning all night."

"You know what rankles me most? That the snake who ratted me out now has my job at the farm labor detail," Johann said.

Helmut nodded. "You need to be more careful. If you haven't realized it before, there's an intricate network of stoolies and informers among us. Men who wouldn't hesitate to sell their own mother if it's to their benefit."

The next day Johann joined his new labor detail and clumped to the mine, brooding. He'd lowered his chances of survival considerably with one careless remark.

Fury snaked through his bony body, leaving a trail of burning behind. Wasn't he even allowed to voice his disgust at the abhorrent conditions he suffered? Naturally, he knew the answer to that question.

I'm not.

He was the enemy, the hateful Nazi, a fascist. It didn't matter that the communists used the same fascist notebook the Nazis had mastered. It didn't matter that the communist *tovarishy*, comrades, doled out the same horrible treatment they condemned in the Nazis. Two different sets of standards existed: one for the Germans and another one for the victors.

And he and his fellow *plenni* were here to repent the sins

their country had committed against the Soviets. They had to atone for all the damages done by Germans during the war.

In that very moment it dawned on him, that the Russians had no intention of letting them go, not until the German slave labor rebuilt their country. Just like they had – and still did – dismantled the German industry and rebuilt it all over the Soviet Union, they had also stolen the able-bodied men of the country, as part of the reparations to be paid.

A groan escaped his throat at the realization and his shoulders sagged some more. The depressing outlook hovered over him and then enveloped him like a cloak of despair. A cosh hit the spot between his shoulders and he yelped.

"*Davai, davai,*" the guard urged him on. Quick, quick.

The detail reached the mine and Johann followed one of the prisoners who'd worked in the mine for a while, imitating his moves. They entered a gallery that became lower with each step. At the end it was less than a yard high and Johann sank to his knees alongside the other pitmen, chopping with the heavy pick against the hard walls of the tunnel.

After mere minutes his hands were burning. Without protective gloves, the skin swelled, and blisters bubbled just to tear open and ooze liquid. After an hour, his hands bled and his slim shoulders cramped with the strain.

Thankfully, the guards never crawled inside the gallery, so he could stretch his shoulders and back every now and then in the confined space at his disposal.

Karl, the leader of the group, took pity on him and said,

"You switch places with Reinhard and bring the coal outside. Pace yourself but walk quickly as soon as the guards can see you."

"Thanks," Johann murmured and squeezed past the man taking his place. The relief lasted only a short moment, because dragging the wheel-less cart with the chipped coal in a crawling position toward the exit proved as strenuous as swinging the pick. At least it offered a bit of respite for the torn skin of his palms.

At the exit he squinted against the blinding sunlight and took a moment to adapt to the light and fully straighten his back. A moment too long.

"*Ugol, ugol, davai, davai!*" Coal, coal, quick, quick, the guard yelled and used his rifle butt to smash Johann's back.

In and out of the gallery he crawled. In with the empty cart, out with a full one so heavy it took him each time more effort to drag it along. Two more times he switched places with Reinhard, changing merely the type of his suffering, but not the intensity.

After nine excruciating hours at the mine, the guards finally called it a day. Johann shuffled homeward, his hands raw and bleeding, his shoulders and back aching, his legs barely capable to sustain his body, and his stomach cramping with hunger.

Almost delirious, he daydreamed about lowering his head into the pigs' trough and stealing their swill. One of the sows approached him with contempt on her face and shoved him away with her snout.

But at the camp only a thin nettle soup and a stale piece of bread waited for him. Immediately after dinner he fell on his bunk, unable to get up again to attend to his other chores.

Half sleeping already he heard Helmut's voice, "Don't worry. I'll do all your chores today."

Johann lasted two weeks and then he collapsed.

CHAPTER 11

J ohann woke in the camp hospital, an overcrowded barracks similar to the others. He was lying in the first ward for the sick people without contagious diseases. There were no medicines or special care, but a Russian doctor came every morning to check on the sick.

"How are you today, *tovarish* Hauser?" the doctor asked him.

"Hungry," Johann croaked.

The doctor glowered at him and pretended not to have heard. He took Johann's temperature, by laying a hand on his forehead, and his pulse. Then he scribbled a note on a list. "You're category four. One week."

Johann looked at the man as he walked down the aisle, deciding in less than a minute about the fate of a man. Category four. A weak smile appeared on Johann's lips. Unsuitable for work. An entire week! That was almost like paradise. A happy summer vacation.

Norbert, the German medic and prisoner himself, stayed busy caring all alone for two hundred sick men. While he didn't slack in his efforts, his results were meager at best. Without equipment the only cure he could offer was clean water and a kind word. He cleaned wounds, washed dirty dressings to re-use them again, and didn't report the dead immediately in order to receive their rations for another day. Without Norbert, many more men would have died.

After three days of bed rest, Johann itched to walk around again. Helmut and Gerd had come to visit him every day for a few minutes, but he still had too much time on his hands to think. And thinking was never good, because it always led to depression.

On the fourth day, he got up to enjoy the late summer sun. By pure accident he ran into a member of the anti-fascist brigade, boasting about the new camp library. Johann wanted to have nothing to do with these people, but after four days of utter boredom and too many depressing thoughts, he followed the man.

The library consisted of a shelf in the room where the political re-education classes were held and boasted a total of twenty books in German: Marx, Engels, Lenin, Stalin and a party program of the newly formed SED, the Socialist Unity Party in the Soviet zone of Germany.

"Light reading," Johann said, his voice dripping with sarcasm. Because of his recent bad experiences with derogatory remarks, he quickly added, "I'll start with Lenin, I think. Isn't he the great mastermind behind the Marxism-Leninism that is the theoretical construct behind the socialism we're privileged to witness as it exists?"

The other prisoner shot him a suspicious glance, but he

couldn't very well chide him for praising the great Lenin.

Johann stayed three weeks in the camp hospital before he was considered fit to work again. His body had used the idle time to recover some of its strength and his mind had honed its sharpness by devouring book after book. The contents might be drab and propagandistic, but the act of reading reached long forgotten corners of his brain. Slowly, Johann's spirit recovered along with his body.

Weeks turned into months and winter returned with a vengeance. He should have been used to the brutal cold by now, but his physical condition had deteriorated more than he'd realized.

Every day was an awful struggle against the bitter, stinging, wet cold that seeped into bones and hearts. The river was frozen, and the prisoners rubbed their hands and faces with snow to get rid of the worst filth. The lice and bedbugs were freezing, too, and made it their mission to crawl into the deepest crevices of the vulnerable men to stay warm.

The itching was maddening, and Johann scratched his skin until it started bleeding. The food supply dried up and became even more meager than last winter. Which was no surprise, because the little news they got from the outside told about a horrible famine all over the Soviet Union. If the Russians didn't have enough to eat themselves, why would they spare food for enemy prisoners?

Shortly before Christmas, a non-event for the communist atheists, a tragedy happened. Gerd stumbled during his work in the lumber mill and the greedy buzz saw neatly sliced off both of his arms. Without proper medical attention Gerd succumbed to his injuries in a matter of hours. But his high-pitched screams followed Johann into his nightmares for weeks.

Just as his two-year anniversary of captivity rolled around, all the men in his barracks were called to the classroom.

"This will be another enlightening lesson about the benefits of the communism," Helmut said, carefully concealing his true opinion.

"At least we can sit and it's warm inside," Johann answered. Sometimes they were bribed with hot water or *kasha*, millet gruel. He hoped today would be one of these days, although he didn't allow himself to get too excited.

"Warm is good. I had frostbite on my nose and cheeks today," Reiner said.

Johann peered at the man. "Seems okay now."

"Yep, the locals shouted at me to rub my face with snow."

"With snow?"

"Weird, right? But it helped. Circulation flowed again and my face is still intact." Reiner grimaced. He wouldn't be the first one to lose the nose, an ear or fingers to the brutal cold.

"Gosh, let's talk about something else," Helmut said, even as they reached the classroom and settled on the chairs.

But instead of the political officer who usually gave the ideological speeches, the camp commandant entered the room, carrying a box. He put the box on the desk in front of him, everyone in the room craning their necks to peer inside.

"Dear God, it's letters," Reiner hissed.

"Letters?" Suddenly Johann's heart raced a mile a minute. Would the two-year period without news from his beloved ones end today? He looked down at his trembling fingers, before his gaze caught Helmut, whose face was white as a ghost, with feverish red dots on his cheeks.

"Nervous?" he asked his friend.

"I so wish my mother is alive."

Johann could barely breathe while the names on the letters were called out.

After an endless time, the official said, "Johann Hauser."

He was completely awestruck and didn't even blink, until Helmut elbowed him and hissed, "That's you. Go!"

Elated, he walked to the front of the room, his gaze fixed on the brown envelope. "Thank you, *gospodin* commandant," he said as the officer handed him the letter. He instantly recognized the handwriting as Lotte's and his heart leapt. *She's alive!*

With trembling hands he removed the single sheet of paper and held it to his face in an attempt to get a whiff of her delicate scent. He traced her handwriting with his fingers, smoothed out the page and began to read –

My dearest Johann,

How happy my heart was to receive news of you. Your friend has stopped by in Berlin on his way to his family. He gave me a wooden doll, which I keep in my purse at all times. It reminds me of you, my darling, and gives me courage.

His hand sank, and he told Helmut, "Karsten arrived safely in Germany."

"Thank God, I was so worried he wouldn't withstand the long journey." Helmut's face showed a genuine smile for the safe arrival of their friend.

"But they took my letter from him."

"That was to be expected. You know how thorough they are in their searches."

Johann nodded, sending grateful thoughts to Karsten for going through the trouble of visiting Lotte and letting her know about Johann's whereabouts. He began reading again.

You can't imagine how worried I was about you. Now at least I know that you're well and alive. Please take care of yourself and stay healthy. I'll be waiting until you return to my side. I know, we never talked about it, and it's a bold move on my part to spell it out, but I honestly wish to spend my life with you.

I returned to Berlin in August 1945 and found that my sisters Anna and Ursula and my mother were still alive. For that I'm incredibly thankful. But what is even better is that our missing brother Richard miraculously turned up at the farm of my aunt.

With the war over, things are slowly returning to normal. So much of Berlin has been destroyed, but everyone works hard to rebuild our beautiful city. Initially I worked as a Trümmerfrau, one of the women clearing the rubble from the streets, but in fall I started my first semester of law studies at the University of Berlin. So far, I like the studies and hope to become a lawyer. My biggest wish is to have you by my side during this exciting yet taxing journey.

I took the liberty of writing a letter to your mother as soon as I received news from you, and I have to tell you that both your parents have died. I'm so sorry, my sweet darling.

Since the day your friend stopped by, I have diligently been writing a letter to you every month, even though the kind lady at the Red Cross told me that despite the best efforts of the Soviet government, distributing the mail to so many prisoners is almost impossible.

In any case, I will continue to write to you, in the hopes that one of my letters will find its way to you. If you can, please write back to me.

Forever yours,

Lotte

Johann's heart swelled reading her lines and he felt tears pricking at his eyes.

Thankfully, one of his fellow prisoners rose to speak. "*Gospodin* commandant, are we allowed to write back?"

The commandant was caught off guard for a moment and glanced around the room into the eyes of two hundred hopeful men. Maybe the combined yearning melted his heart, because he said, "Of course. I'll have postcards distributed tonight."

Indeed, later in the evening the guards distributed one postcard to every man with instructions to write a maximum of fifty words and only positive things.

"What the hell do they expect me to write then?" Johann complained.

"About the weather, maybe?" Reiner offered.

"Write to your girl how happy you are about her letter and that you think of her every day," Helmut suggested.

Johann furrowed his brow. It should be easy enough to tell Lotte how much he loved her and mirror her sentiments about wanting to return to her side. But a nagging thought held him back.

While his comrades scribbled the allotted fifty words on their postcards, he stared holes into the air.

"What's wrong?" Helmut asked.

"Nothing."

"Aha." Helmut poked him in the arm, where once a biceps had been. "Then why is your postcard still empty?"

"It's just…" Johann sighed. "What if she doesn't want me anymore?"

Helmut's face showed alarm. "Did she say so?"

"Not really… but…"

"What did she say in her letter?"

"That she loves me…"

Reiner joined the conversation. "And how, exactly, does this imply she doesn't want you anymore?"

"I'm a millstone around her neck."

Both his friends stared at him wide-eyed, until Helmut demanded, "Let me read her letter."

Wordlessly, Johann handed it over, biting his lips as Helmut's eyes scanned the text. His friend would see the hidden threat, wouldn't he? Johann was so much beneath her; she'd run away screaming once she realized the truth.

"Holy shit!" Helmut exclaimed.

"What is it?" Reiner and another bunk neighbor asked curiously.

"She's basically proposing marriage." Helmut returned the letter and faced Johann. "That woman is madly in love with you."

"Yes… but… didn't you read the part about her studying law?"

His friend nodded. "I did. What's so bad about it?"

Johann hid his face in his hands. "She'll be a lawyer, and I? A slave worker who hasn't learned anything but the trade of a soldier."

"Seriously?" Reiner asked.

Johann nodded.

"If she holds this against you, she isn't worth shit," Heinz said.

"Look. You were a Leutnant in the Wehrmacht, that is something," Helmut said.

"Former Wehrmacht soldiers aren't exactly popular right now." Johann wanted to believe them, but how could he? Lotte wouldn't want to be dragged down by someone like him. She might believe so right now, because she was blinded by her infatuation and the sweet times they'd shared in Warsaw. But once she faced reality, she'd turn away from him, disgusted. "Have you recently had a good look at me? At any one of us?"

"Nothing a shower and good food every day can't fix," Helmut said lightly. "And when we return home— "

"If," Johann interrupted him.

"When, not if." Helmut fixed his gaze successively on the three men. "When we return home, each of us will start a new life. We'll do it with the same tenacity that we're now using to hang on for dear life. You, Johann, can learn a new vocation or go to university. Anything is possible. Civilian life back home will be so much easier than what we experience now, and that is our advantage. We won't complain how hard it is to get up at 5 a.m...." The men nodded and grinned. "...or that it's too hard to study at night, or carry a heavy load, or even that it's too cold to go outside."

Johann had never seen anything positive in his captivity, but the way Helmut painted it, it didn't sound all that bad. He wished he had the unwavering optimism his friend possessed.

"Okay, I'll write to her," he said it with a smile, already

dreaming about how her soft curves felt pressed against his body.

CHAPTER 12

Voronezh, June 1947

The awful winter passed, but this time spring didn't bring the desperately awaited relief. A horrible famine held Russia in its grip. Locals starved and the *plenni* died like flies.

"Every day they're giving us less food and making us work more!" Johann grumbled, looking at the bowl of soup in his hand. Soup was a euphemistic expression for the hot water in the bowl. Not nearly enough to take the edge off his gnawing hunger, even after adding dandelions and moss he'd picked on the way to work.

"It's a small sacrifice to pay for the glorious days ahead once communism takes hold," one of the informers chastised him.

Johann glowered at the soup bowl, but remembering the

harsh lesson for dissent, he schooled his voice and answered, "You're right. But it's still hard."

"Nobody said it would be child's play. We have to transform an entire country and educate millions of people. Naturally, there will be some hiccups."

Johann didn't consider the worst famine in a decade a hiccup, but serious mismanagement on the part of the communists. Wise from experience, he didn't voice his thoughts.

"Any idea how long until we're privy to a new and better world?" Reiner muttered.

The informer glowered at him and said, "Not long until our sacrifices will be rewarded plentifully."

Once the informer left, and only Johann, Reiner and Helmut sat around, Johann said, "Sounds a lot like the Bible. Repent now for an uncertain better future that is far, far away."

Helmut sighed. "Even though you might not see the difference, because your heart is bitter, there is a huge difference between God's message and communism. For one, God is benign and wants us to love our neighbor as we love ourselves, whereas the communists want you to denounce him."

"Don't let the communists hear your blasphemy against their God, Stalin."

"I always wonder whether the newly converted antifaboys really believe this shit," Reiner said. "Or do they simply play by the rulebook?"

Johann gave a bitter grimace. "Given that the Soviet interpretation of communism is nothing but a badly disguised copy of National Socialism, I tend to believe the former believers found a new religion."

"And since when are you the expert on communism?" Helmut asked.

"Since I read all twenty books in the camp library about that topic."

"You did? Why on earth?" Reiner said.

Johann scoffed. "Because those were the only books our wonderful library owns. And I was bored... not having to work while classified four is a blessing and a curse. You lie in bed all day and while your body recovers, your brain idles along going down very unpleasant lanes... so reading communist trash was better than thinking of the ways those bastards are going to kill me without even lifting a finger."

"Shush. If they hear you..." Reiner hushed him.

"See? We can't even speak our mind. Isn't that exactly the same as under Nazi rule? The same retaliation for dissent? Letting people starve and working them to death in camps? The only thing the Soviets are not doing are the mass shootings, and do you know why?"

His friends had become paler with each word, but he ignored their frightened faces.

"I'll tell you why! Because they need our manpower to rebuild their rotten country. They could get so much more work done, if they treated us well! But that's not their intent. They want us dead, all of us. And while they do away with us, they first suck out every last drop of blood from our bodies like those damn mosquitoes do."

"You're upset..." Helmut tried to appease him, but Johann couldn't hold back any longer. The anger, the pain, the disappointed hopes, it had been boiling inside for much too long and needed an outlet.

"I'm upset and rightly so! What they're doing are war crimes."

"We're not at war anymore…" Reiner said.

"See? The bloody war stopped two years ago and we're still here. And you know what? I'm ashamed."

"Ashamed of what?" A man who'd joined the antifa-brigade had entered the room.

Johann didn't care. He glowered at him, "Ashamed that I once believed in Hitler and his idea of making Germany great again. How could I not see how this would end? How could I not make out the first signs of warning? How could I let all those horrible things happen and not stand up to stop them? Why was I so stupid?"

The antifa-man gave a puzzled look and said, "So why don't you join the antifa-brigade if this is how you think?"

Yes, why? Johann was too afraid to tell the man that communism was just another form of fascism, and he hated himself for being so cowardly – again. "Because I'm afraid to make another mistake."

"So you don't believe anti-fascism is good?"

"I certainly believe fascism is bad." Johann didn't want to get into hot water again and tried to appease the man.

Thankfully the call to head into the barracks for the night cut the conversation short.

CHAPTER 13

Berlin, September 1947

Lotte's oldest sister Ursula had married this past spring and moved out of the apartment to live with her husband, Tom. Mother and Father, the latter who'd returned a wreck last fall after four years in Russian captivity, had left the horrible living conditions in Berlin and moved to Bavaria.

Now only Lotte and her second sister Anna remained in Berlin. But Anna was so occupied with her work, and her husband, she barely had time for Lotte, even before she became pregnant. While Lotte didn't begrudge her sisters their happiness, she often felt lonely and abandoned.

It didn't help that her friends at university urged her to move on and live her life. Their words nagged at her head and heart.

*The war's over and you're young, you have to enjoy yourself.
Why don't you come with us to the dance? Let's go and have some
fun. We can meet some GIs and have them take us out.*

With her twenty-first birthday coming up next week,
she suddenly felt old. All the other girls at university were
either dating or already married. Some looked at her with
pity, others with disbelief, already calling her an old spin-
ster behind her back.

It had been almost three years since she'd last seen
Johann. And while her heart didn't doubt her love for him,
her mind oftentimes pleaded with her to follow the advice
of her classmates and move on.

Eighteen months ago, Karsten had visited to bring her
news of Johann's whereabouts. Eighteen letters she'd
written and given to the Red Cross. And she still hadn't
received an answer. She was running out of hope.

A single tear rolled down her cheek. More and more
men – sick, broken shells of men – returned home from
Russian captivity. All of them had similar stories to tell, if
they talked at all, and none of the things they said gave her
the reassurance she craved.

It would be a miracle if Johann were still alive. How
long could a man withstand backbreaking slave labor on
next to no food? A year? Or two? Four years like her
father?

She sighed and packed her things to leave for university.

"Hi, Lotte, what's up?" Dietrich, a classmate, sidled up to
her at the entrance to the building.

"Not much. Scavenging for food when I'm not studying."

"Doesn't your mother do this?"

"She's not in Berlin."

"Oh. I couldn't imagine doing anything in addition to my studies. It's so time-consuming already," he complained.

Of course you can't, because you're a man and the women in your family shoulder all the burdens, she thought, slightly annoyed.

"There's a group of us going to a dance on the weekend. Would you come with me?" he said just before they reached the lecture hall.

"Dietrich, thank you for the invitation, but I'm afraid I wouldn't be good company. My heart already belongs to someone else."

His eyes narrowed. "Really? I never see you with anyone."

It reared its ugly head again, her need to justify why she was saving herself for a man who might never return. "That's because he's still a prisoner of war."

"After such a long time? And you're sure he's still alive?"

"No, I'm not! But as long as I have hope in my heart, I won't date another man," she spat out the words, not caring about his wounded expression.

She searched for a familiar face in the lecture hall. One of her friends waved her over and Lotte eagerly left Dietrich's side.

"Hey, Lotte. Did Dietrich ask you out?" Marlene asked.

"Yes." Lotte unpacked her bag and stacked a notepad and pencil on the desk in front of her.

"And... what did you say?"

Lotte gave a snort. "I declined, of course."

"You didn't!" Marlene gazed at her with wide-open eyes. "Of course you did. It's plain crazy to keep waiting for that soldier of yours. How long were you even together?"

"Three months." That was actually quite generous, because during that time the Warsaw Uprising had taken place, separating them for a considerable amount of time.

"Three months!" Marlene squealed. "You walked with him for three months and now you think you owe him eternal fidelity? What if he returns and the two of you don't even recognize each other anymore? Those things happen, you know? Then you'll have thrown away years of your youth."

Lotte pursed her lips. "Hitler and the Nazis stole most of my youth, and it's not like I'm not enjoying myself…" She wanted to say more, but the professor entered the lecture hall and all conversation fell silent.

Despite confidence in her feelings for Johann, a nagging thought remained. Was it possible that they'd drifted apart, and she clung to an image of him that didn't exist anymore? So much had happened, and she'd changed since they'd last seen each other. He must have changed, too. Was their love strong enough to pick up from where they'd left off?

Suddenly she sensed the tick-tock of a clock. Every passing second took her further away from Johann.

Tick-tock.

Tick-tock.

No! Johann would return to her side. Wasn't that what the crazy old woman in Denmark had predicted? Lotte wasn't superstitious, didn't believe in witchcraft, but the more time passed, the more she clung to Ingrid's words, wanting them to be true. *He will return. Yes, he will.*

After university she queued for food, doing her homework while standing in line. As she walked to the apartment, she noticed that Berlin was slowly starting to look more like a city than a war zone. Pride filled her heart. She'd done her bit to make this change happen when toiling as a *Trümmerfrau* for months before she took up her studies. Even now she worked on weekends to add to the meager rations she received as a student.

Thankfully she didn't have to worry about rent, because Anna and Peter both worked and had offered to shoulder this burden, so Lotte could dedicate more time to her studies.

When she unlocked the door and entered the apartment, she saw her sister making out with Peter on the sofa. They were so caught up in each other that they didn't notice her. Lotte stared at them with envy for a moment, before she turned around and closed the door – loudly. Then she took plenty of time removing her coat and gloves and putting her worn-out shoes next to Anna's.

When she entered the living room, Peter and Anna sat on the sofa as if nothing had happened. But Lotte wasn't fooled. Anna's bright rosy cheeks and the glimmer in her blue eyes betrayed her.

"Hi, Anna, Peter, is dinner in the kitchen?" she asked as casually as possible.

"Oh, I, we… we just got home and we both ate at work," Anna said, smoothing down her skirt. "Shall I prepare something for you?"

"No. I'll just grab a piece of bread." Lotte smiled. "Where's Jan?"

Peter grinned. "Officially out with friends. He won't be home before eight."

"Officially?"

"He's sweet on a girl," Anna explained about Peter's

fifteen-year-old son.

"Oh." Lotte fled into the kitchen before her feelings could overwhelm her. The entire world seemed populated by happy couples – except for her.

A postcard with a Red Cross stamp on it lay on the kitchen table. Her heart beat wildly and she couldn't breathe. Trembling, she approached the table, fully expecting the postcard to disintegrate in front of her eyes – a mere figment of her imagination.

But it lay still. Unmoving. Lotte sneaked up on it and snatched it. It had her name on it. In *his* handwriting. Shakier than she remembered, but unmistakably his. She flopped onto the chair, holding the postcard to her heart for several long moments. Then she raised it to her eyes and read.

Dearest Lotte,

Your letter brought me so much joy, knowing that you're still mine. I'm well and alive. Obviously, I'm missing you, but otherwise I'm fine and I hope to be released soon. I cannot wait to hold you in my arms again. Sending you kisses.

Love forever,

Johann

The tears rolled down her cheeks and she croaked, "Anna! Come!"

Anna rushed into the kitchen and asked, full of worry, "What's wrong?"

"A postcard. From Johann."

"Oh, dear." Anna wrapped her arms around Lotte, holding her close. "That's such good news."

CHAPTER 14

The *plenni* lived in a constant rollercoaster of hope and disappointment that added to the physical hardships, and more than one of the men went off the rails.

Some recovered after a few days in the camp hospital, while others took desperate measures. They stepped out of the line during their walk to work, knowing full well the guards would shoot them without hesitation.

One morning, commanders of the MVD, the Ministry of Internal Affairs, showed up at the camp. Their arrival struck fear into prisoners and guards alike, because the MVD was formerly known as the NKVD, or Soviet secret police – an organization comparable to the sinister Gestapo.

"These guys are bad news," Helmut said after roll call.

"Why are they here?"

"No idea. Watch your mouth, will you?"

Johann nodded and clumped off to work. When his labor detail returned eleven hours later, a strange tension had settled over the camp. He bumped into one of the antifa-boys and asked him, "What's going on?"

"They've been hauling prisoners into their interrogation rooms all day long."

"Interrogation rooms?"

"Yeah."

"What for?"

"Nobody knows."

"Prisoner Hauser, come with me!" A guard had spotted Johann and made a check on some list in his hands.

A shiver ran down Johann's spine. No doubt he'd be interrogated by the MVD. But what for? What did they want? Johann had worked in an office during most of the war, organizing logistics to and from the front. Only in the last months of the war had he been thrown into active combat.

He entered a small room in the administration office with only four chairs and a table. Two of the chairs were occupied by well-fed men in uniform.

"Sit down," the older one told him.

Johann obeyed. As soon as he settled into the chair, the door opened again, and an attractive young woman entered. She sauntered toward Johann, apparently oblivious to the MVD commanders at the table. Unwillingly he held his breath, waiting for the inevitable rebuke.

"Good evening, Leutnant Hauser. My name is Olga Saltanova. Commander Toporov has a few questions he would like you to answer and I have the honor to be your translator," she said with a smile.

"*Tovarish* Saltanova," he stuttered.

"No, please call me Olga." She extended her manicured hand.

"Olga." Dumbfounded, he took her hand and inhaled her exquisite perfume. Her face was round and rosy with high cheekbones and beautiful brown eyes. But his eyes didn't rest for long on her elaborate makeup. They were automatically drawn downward to her generous cleavage, which showcased her full and plump breasts.

He hadn't seen such a beautiful, and alluring woman in years and the sight of her bustline, combined with the heavy perfume, made him dizzy. He caught himself just in time before he licked his dry lips and much to his distress, he noticed a long-forgotten tingle in his pants.

Commander Toporov asked something in Russian, but Johann had forgotten all about his language skills, his eyes riveted to the line where Olga's breasts met.

"The commander would like to know if you ever shot civilians during your time in the Wehrmacht?" she translated Toporov's words.

Johann tore his gaze away from her and looked at the commander. "*Gospodin* Commander. No. I never shot at civilians."

Olga translated his answer and then waited while another question was asked. Whether he wanted to or not, he had to look at her face when she addressed him again. "How many houses of peace-loving civilians have you burned down?"

"I've never done anything like that," Johann replied.

The interrogation continued for two hours, repeating over and over the same questions. It became increasingly difficult to focus on his answers, because every time he looked at Olga, his manly parts twitched and tingled. After years without seeing a woman, except for the doctor, nearby, he simply couldn't control his reactions to a plump breast all but shoved into his face.

"What other atrocities did you commit against peace-loving Russian civilians?" Olga asked.

"I never even set foot into Russia before I was brought here as prisoner."

The commander's face twitched, and he exchanged a few words with Olga. Johann got the impression that the commander actually understood German quite well and didn't need a translator. Olga was here for the sole reason of distracting him and making him slip up.

He vowed to be even more careful with every word he said. It wouldn't be the first time the Soviets took a sentence out of context and switched around the meaning.

"So you admit to having committed crimes against civilians of other nationalities?" Olga said.

"No. I never harmed a civilian, Russian or otherwise." Johann's eyelids threatened to close with exhaustion. He hadn't even had dinner and could only hope that Helmut had saved him up a bowl of soup. He grimaced at the thought. The hot soup tasted like bitter dishwater, but cold soup was so much worse.

"Did you grimace because you remembered the awful crimes you perpetrated against peace-loving civilians?"

"No. I didn't," Johann burst out, but sagged in the same moment. If they noticed his tension, they'd have him right where they wanted him. "I grimaced because I missed dinner and my stomach is hurting."

The commander pursed his lips and said, "You can eat as

much as you want, if you decide to finally tell us the truth and confess your crimes."

Johann blanked his expression of all emotion, although anger roiled through his body. The promise was alluring. Eat until he was full for the first time in more than two years? He'd forgotten how it felt not to be hungry. The temptation overwhelmed Johann, but would he sign his own death sentence when he told them what they wanted to hear?

He sighed. "*Gospodin* Commander, I have told you the truth the entire time. I never committed any crimes against civilians. I fought other soldiers, because our countries were at war."

Olga repeated his answer and the commander slammed his hand down on the table, shooting angry stares at her. Johann almost felt sorry for her, because she apparently would get into trouble for not teasing a confession out of him.

"Commander Toporov wants to know why you persist in telling us these lies. You seem to believe you are very clever, but the commander wants you to know that in the end he will make you talk."

What were they after? Did it make a difference if he said what they wanted to hear? Was there a worse hell than this camp? Or a quick and painless death? Torture? The icy grip of fear crushed Johann's spirit. *Not torture, please.* He was tempted to offer the commander the compromise that he'd work in the coal mine instead. Anything but torture.

"I did nothing wrong," Johann said, exhaustion making his brain slow to react. His eyelids drooped. Someone prodded his arm.

Olga smiled at him, leaning over to give him a very good view at her precious boobs. "Commander Toporov wants you to know that if you don't cooperate, you will never see a naked woman again and will certainly never fuck one."

Johann felt himself flush at her words, but she didn't flinch the tiniest bit. More pleasant thoughts that involved his hands on a naked woman wiped away his exhaustion. Reveling in his daydreams, he was caught unawares at the next question and understood only part of it. "I'm sorry. Can you repeat that, I didn't..."

The commander slammed his hand on the table again.

Olga listened for a moment and then translated, "Commander Toporov will not repeat the question. He wants to know if you are admitting it?"

"Admitting what? I didn't do anything. I didn't even understand your question," Johann replied. The righteous anger fueled his brain. They'd tricked him with sex, lowering his guard. He had to be more alert.

The questions continued. On and on... until the commander said, "I'm hungry. You can return to your barracks. For now."

Johann clearly understood the thinly veiled threat, but at this point he didn't care anymore.

Everyone in the barracks was already fast asleep, but Helmut woke when Johann slid into the bunk.

"Is that you, Johann?" Helmut whispered from the neighboring bunk.

"Yes."

"I saved you dinner."

Tears welled in Johann's eyes as Helmut slid from his

bed and removed a mug with soup and a piece of bread that he'd hidden under the bunk.

"You're a saint," Johann said, greedily devouring the food in the darkness of the barracks.

"What did they want?"

"They kept prodding me to admit to war crimes."

"I've heard as much. They're keen on anyone above the rank of a foot soldier."

"Silence!" someone yelled.

Johann swallowed the rest of his food, plummeted onto his bunk and fell asleep before his head hit the hard mattress.

Over the next week the Russians interrogated him a total of ten times. Each time they asked the same questions, and each time he gave the same answers. By the time Johann left the interrogation room on the seventh day, he was more determined than ever to make sure Commander Toporov never extracted any sort of confession from him.

CHAPTER 15

A gain, rumors spread like wildfire. But as always, the
Russians promised the moon and delivered nothing.
Johann didn't get his hopes up anymore, because nothing
was worse than the resulting disappointment. So, he didn't
pay attention to the newest talk about *Heimkehrer*
transports.

But then one evening Helmut came rushing to him and
yelled, "We're all going home!"

It took Johann a few moments to process the information, but then a huge grin spread across his face. "It's for real
this time?"

"They say the camp will be closed and everyone sent
home," Reiner added.

"You think it's true?" Johann asked.

"One can never be sure, but the commandant himself
said that by Christmas this year everyone will be home. Not
only our camp, but every single POW who's still in Russia."

"By Christmas?" Johann's face took on a wistful expression. It was only spring, but with the prospect of going home, he could hang on some more months.

"That's what he said."

The next morning during roll call, the rumors were confirmed. The commandant gave a short speech about the virtues of communism and how they needed good people in Eastern Germany to help rebuild the country.

Johann squinted his eyes. He didn't like the implications one bit. His last residence had been in Munich, now in the American zone, and he didn't know anyone in the Soviet sector.

"We're organizing three transports and sending everyone home – everyone who's still in the camps in our great Soviet Union, even SS, police, and officers, everyone at all. You will all spend Christmas with your families," the commandant said.

Every single *plenni* in the camp hung on the commandant's words, soaking up the promise of freedom. It was like an energy boost, and a humming tension filled the air.

But the very next day the commandant's deputy put a damper on their joy. "...if you want to go home, you need to become a best-worker first!"

The collective shock in the camp cut the air like a whip. Suddenly everyone stood straighter.

"A best-worker?" Helmut groaned. "Aren't they exploiting us enough already?"

"Apparently not," Johann whispered back.

In the following days, the men worked even harder than usual, doing everything to become best-workers and earning their transfer home. The carrot dangling in front of their noses, they forced their haggard bodies to work longer and harder than ever before. Many men passed out from the superhuman efforts and, sadly, some didn't live to earn the title of best-workers.

About a week later, when Johann returned from his work detail, Helmut came rushing toward him. "We're on the list! We're on the list!"

Johann fell into the arms of his friend, and one by one his comrades told the same good news. A collective sigh went through the camp. This time the Russians would keep their promise. They would all go home to their families.

Johann dreamt about Lotte. Walking with her hand in hand. Drinking a beer. Eating food until his stomach was full. Taking her to bed and finally making love to her again. A tear threatened to spill down his cheek and he quickly blinked it away.

"What will you do first when you get home?" Helmut asked him.

Johann grinned. "Kiss my girl."

That comment drew similar remarks from a number of the men, and sobering comments from others. Men who hadn't received notes from the loved ones they had left behind. Men who didn't know if they had families left to go home to.

The next day everyone on the *Heimkehrer* list received new clothing: a dark blue padded jacket, blue fatigues and a blue shirt. But before putting them on, the men had to endure the delousing procedure.

Naturally, nobody complained, and Johann relished the feeling of being bug-free. He put on the brand-new clothing and gave a sigh of relief. It was such a joy to wear soft and clean things.

Now all they had to do was wait. The first transport was supposed to leave within forty-eight hours. Giddy with anticipation, Johann sorted his meager belongings.

Lotte's photograph was always in his breast pocket. He ran his finger across her face and whispered, "Soon, I'll be with you, my love. Very soon." He put the photo into the pocket of his new shirt.

A frightening thought occurred to him. He'd find Lotte, and then what? He didn't have a job, had never learned anything apart from being a soldier. Without being able to provide for her, he couldn't even ask her to marry him. Shock settled deep down in his soul as he realized he'd have to start his new life from zero again.

Nothing was ever going to be the same.

He willed the worrisome thoughts away and meticulously checked his other belongings: the tin mug for soup, a knife carved out of wood in many nights' work, an extra pair of socks and a woolen undershirt. That was all. He decided to keep the knife as a reminder but would give away everything else to a needy comrade. Who knew how long before the second transport left the camp? They sure could use the extra stuff.

Those not on the list stared with unconcealed envy at the lucky men in the shiny, new clothes. While Johann felt sorry for them, he couldn't stop grinning at his own good fortune in returning home soon.

Skoro domoi.

CHAPTER 16

The next morning a messenger rushed up to Johann. "You shall report to the office immediately."

"What for?"

"Don't know, but you're not the only one." The messenger dashed off to bring the order to more men.

Johann sighed and walked to the office building. What could they want from him now? His stomach clenched as he stepped into the office, where two Soviet officers waited for him. They took his personal data and compared it against the list lying on the desk.

"Take off your new returnee clothes," the younger officer said.

Johann's heart plummeted into his shoes. "What?"

"Over there are other clothes, but hurry up, we don't have much time."

It didn't make sense to oppose their commands, so Johann took off his clean and shiny new clothes and slipped into the old, stinking, bug-infested rags they'd laid out for him. In the last moment he remembered to rescue Lotte's photograph and the wooden knife from his pockets.

When he was ready, the senior officer showed him a piece of paper and read the text to Johann – in Russian. The younger officer translated, "You are arrested."

Johann was rendered speechless. How could they arrest him, since he already was a prisoner? The translator hadn't mentioned on what grounds they were arresting him, and Johann didn't dare ask.

"*Davai, davai,*" they rushed him on.

Outside in the yard, his joyful comrades didn't dare wave or even look at him. None of them wanted to be affiliated with him, for fear of being taken away, too, and losing the ticket to the transport home.

Johann had never felt more humiliated or abandoned than while running the gauntlet past his former comrades. Only Helmut, who lingered near the exit gates, caught Johann's gaze for a moment and voiced a silent, "God help you".

He balled his fist. God had long ago abandoned him. Him and every other man rotting away in the Russian camps.

The Soviet officers shoved him into the back of a police car where other *plenni* with desolate expressions on their faces were already waiting. Two soldiers with rifles and two snarling and growling bloodhounds guarded them. The dogs growled at the slightest movement of the men and he had no doubt they'd mangle him to shreds.

The police car drove at breakneck speed into the center of Voronezh. Johann recognized some of the buildings that he and his fellow *plenni* had constructed with little more than their bare hands. The car stopped in front of the prison building. Johann and his fellows were shoved out and taken inside.

Even after so many years in captivity, a shiver of fear ran down Johann's spine at the sound of the door falling shut behind him. His legs filled with lead and he could barely drag himself along.

The camp had been hell, but the concrete prison building with barred windows invoked instant claustrophobia. Two guards pushed each of the prisoners into an empty cell and locked the door behind them. Johann was left alone with his fear-stricken thoughts.

It didn't take long until the door opened again, and two female guards entered his cell. One of them stood by and watched, while the other one thoroughly shook him down.

She found the wooden knife in his pocket and seized it. Then her fingers reached the picture in his breast pocket and his heart stopped beating. The Russians had a thorough disdain for paper in the hands of the prisoners, afraid they could write down something negative about their great country. Paper was always confiscated when found and if the guards found scribbled notes on a *plenni*, they often punished him for the transgression.

The guard removed Lotte's picture and gazed at it, asking, "Woman, you?"

"Yes, this is my girlfriend," he answered and then pleaded, "Please, don't take it away."

The two guards conversed in Russian, and turned over the picture several times, scrutinizing it. When they didn't find a single word written on it, the older one nodded and said, "He can keep it. Give it back."

A stone the size of the Ural Mountains fell from his shoulders when the guard who'd shaken him down returned Lotte's picture to his breast pocket. He all but sagged in relief. But the search wasn't over yet.

The guard standing to the back ordered, "Take off your clothes."

Having experienced the embarrassing ass-squeezing medical exams on a regular basis, he didn't even hesitate to follow her commands. There wasn't much dignity left that the Russians hadn't violated already.

He hadn't seen himself in a mirror for years, had even avoided glancing down his limbs, terrified of the horrific sight.

All the *plenni* in the camp looked like walking skeletons, the leathery skin hanging down in flaps. There was no flesh to round out the skin, no muscle to stretch it. The skin of every man in the camp had a different shade of gray, from the pale whitish-gray of ashes in winter to the darkened gray of those working outside all day in summer. The sick had varying shades of yellow-gray or green-gray. And the dead turned a black-gray if they weren't buried fast enough.

He undressed in front of the women and neatly folded the rags that were his clothes, before he put them on the floor. The guard searched his naked body with the same diligence she'd searched his clothes. Did she expect him to be hiding something between the loose flaps of his skin?

She looked into his ears, checked his nose and his mouth. Then she continued her search with his private parts. For a moment, anger flared up in his tired bones, but the emotion disappeared as fast as it had come. During his years in captivity he'd learned to save his energy for things that mattered. Someone checking beneath the uncut hood of his penis wasn't worth losing precious calories over.

He stood like a puppet on strings, enduring whatever they did to his body. It didn't make sense to protest, or even to feel humiliated. In the eyes of these women he wasn't a man. He was but a *wojenno plenni*, a prisoner of war, the lowest kind of prisoner. Even the pigs, the mules and the cows stood way above him in the hierarchy.

Germany had lost the war. Surrendered unconditionally. The Soviets belonged to the winners and could treat him however they wished.

"You can dress again."

The command gave the awaited redemption and Johann dressed again under the vigilant eyes of his two guards. They led him to another cell that was already occupied by nine bedraggled men. Some of them he recognized from the camp, but others seemed to be common Russian criminals.

Johann found a space against the wall and huddled into a ball. He had no desire to talk to anyone. Worries whirled around his head and he tried hard to push them away. It didn't work. After a while, he glanced up, annoyed. The breathing, coughing and groaning of the other men was a nuisance.

By now he should have gotten used to the lack of privacy, but alas, that wasn't the case. He wished for just an hour to himself, with nobody present to witness his misery.

CHAPTER 17

A day passed, then two, then a week and Johann still had no idea why he was in prison. But he knew that the transport home had left without him.

He and the others were constantly transferred from one overcrowded cell to the next one. More unfortunate Germans were brought to the prison and with the news they shared, the puzzle in his head started to form a clear picture.

The first transport, in fact, had left the camp with both Reiner and Helmut on it. As much as Johann was happy on their behalf, he also felt the sting of loneliness. Deprived of his two close friends his future looked even bleaker.

Apparently, the arrest had something to do with the interrogations by the MVD a while back. Johann thought he'd fared quite well, not admitting to any of the crimes he'd been asked about many times. But who knew?

Being confined in the prison cell gnawed at his intestines and he missed the relative freedom of the camp.

Going outside. Seeing the sky. Moving about without stumbling over the limbs of other prisoners. The only silver lining was that he didn't have to work. It made the meager rations look slightly less daunting. But the idleness was a double-edged sword, because it gave Johann's brain time to think – and worry.

He worried day in, day out, racking his brain for a clue about why he was there. Until on the seventh day of his arrest the guards took him from his cell.

"Today's your trial," the guard said, shoving him into the back of a police car with a handful of other *plenni*.

"Where are you taking us?" Johann asked, but the guard had already locked the door.

About twenty minutes later, the car stopped in front of the MVD building, another concrete monster built with the blood and sacrifice of German POWs. Usually Johann would have grinned at the irony, but he was way beyond feeling anything but trepidation.

Upon arrival, the men were separated and placed in small two-by-two-yard cells. More endless hours of waiting began. Johann slumped on the floor, unable to keep the demons from attacking his soul. In an effort to stay sane, he forced himself to scrutinize the cell and noticed scribbling on the walls.

He got up, approached one of the inscriptions and deciphered *Harald Krupp, 25 years*. Suspicion invaded his soul and he walked over to the next note scratched into the wall. *Fritz Berger, 25 years*. Dizziness threatened to overwhelm him as he began to understand. Frantically he seared for more scribbled testimonies. *Martin Becker, 25 years. Heinz Langer, 25 years. Konrad Maier, 25 years.*

Twenty-five years! Every single one of his unfortunate predecessors had been given a sentence of twenty-five years. Johann's legs gave out and he sank to the floor, screaming out his fear, his anguish, and his despair. It all came spewing forth until his voice was hoarse and only cracked whispers erupted from his throat.

His life lay spread out in front of him. A good Wehrmacht soldier, following orders. He wasn't an angel, because no man with a weapon in his hand could be called that, but he'd drawn a line where civilians were concerned.

Like most of the Wehrmacht, he felt a stark disdain for the Waffen-SS and their atrocious behavior. He closed his eyes at the awful memories of the events in Baluty. His unit was tasked with retaliating against a village of partisans for blowing up a bridge. They gathered all the males in the village. Bile rose in his throat as he relived the gruesome scene. The SS arrived, and he pulled out his own men with some pretense, but it was too late. They all witnessed the killing of every one of the village menfolk.

That was the day he finally stopped believing in Hitler and his war. Nothing justified the atrocities committed.

Shame rose in Johann. He couldn't absolve himself of guilt. He had been a staunch believer in Nazism from the very beginning. Hitler's promise to make Germany great again after the unjust Treaty of Versailles had been fuel to a nation's wounded pride and Johann had fallen for it. He'd fallen for the racist ideology and the fraudulent scheme of making the Jews the scapegoat for all the evil in the world.

His ears burned with shame as he reminisced. The great master race had lost the war and the inferior subhuman Russians now held the upper hand. Wasn't this proof enough for the ridiculousness of the notion of racial superiority?

And hadn't Eden proven that Jews could be kind and compassionate? When everyone else had dropped him like a hot potato, she'd been the only one to help, despite knowing that he was a Nazi and hated her kind. But she'd been committed to the truth, nothing else. And he'd never been able to offer her his thanks. *I hope she survived the war.*

Was this trial God's punishment for sins committed?

Johann pushed the frightening thoughts aside, and his mind wandered to his dead parents and then to Lotte. In his loneliness, he relived each moment they had spent together like a slow-playing motion picture in his head.

Lotte had stolen his heart from the first moment he'd met her. Thinking about her sweet face and the soft feel of her lips on his own brought a smile to his face. For her he had to be strong.

The door opened and a guard said, "Come. Your trial is on."

Johann followed the guard through endless hallways until they reached the courtroom. At the front stood a large table covered with a bright red tablecloth. Behind the table sat three uniformed Soviet officers, projecting an air of authority.

On the left side of the table sat a man and on the right side a woman with a typewriter in front of her, presumably the court reporter. There were no other people in the room, apart from him and the guard. And no chairs.

Johann approached the table, unsure what he was supposed to do.

The most senior officer, with the insignia of a captain, began talking and after each sentence, the man on the left side of the table translated. First, they asked for his personal information and if he understood the charges.

"I don't," Johann said.

"Do you want a defender?"

"Yes."

"There is a fee involved." The translator shuffled his papers and said, "It's one thousand rubles."

Johann bit back a sarcastic remark. Everything in the Soviet economy had a fee involved. At the beginning of the year, the *plenni* had first received a *salary* for their work. In good months it amounted to one thousand rubles, but only a maximum of one hundred fifty rubles was paid out to the prisoner. The rest was spent on taxes and for food and accommodation in the camp – a great scheme to press out even more work from the prisoners with the lure of letting them keep some money to buy essentials like food or a warm blanket.

"Then I will have to defend myself," Johann said.

"If this is your wish."

It's not my wish but you bloody bastards don't give me a choice.

"Captain Gorky will now read the accusations levied against you," the translator explained and then translated the captain's words.

"You are charged on two counts: murdering the peace-loving Soviet civilians and stealing from the peace-loving Soviet civilians."

Johann suppressed an angry hiss. Those were the same accusations that damn Commander Toporov had thrown at him dozens of times. "I have never done any such thing. Before being captured in Warsaw, I'd never even set foot in the Soviet Union."

"Poland is part of the great communist empire and as such all crimes committed against the peace-loving Polish civilians are considered crimes against the Soviet people," the translator said. "So, do you admit to terrorizing the peace-loving Soviet population?"

"I do not. I never terrorized civilians."

"It has come to the court's attention that you participated in the massacre of Baluty. Is that correct?"

"No." Johann paled. In a moment of inadvertence at the camp he'd talked about the awful massacre he'd witnessed. Apparently one of the listeners had been an informer with nothing better to do than rat Johann out.

"So you never were in Baluty?"

"I was. But my unit pulled out as soon as the SS began killing the village people."

"You did nothing to stop them from killing innocent and peace-loving villagers?"

Johann sighed. "I couldn't do anything. My rank didn't allow me..."

"Enough. You stood by and watched your countrymen slaughter innocent people." A short conversation in Russian ensued and at the end the translator announced, "The court finds you guilty as charged of murdering peace-loving Soviet civilians."

The second charge, for stealing, followed a similar line of reasoning. Because Johann had eaten meat during his time in Warsaw, he was found guilty of having stolen pigs from the Polish farmers.

It probably didn't matter. What difference did stealing make when he'd already been found guilty of murder?

The so-called trial lasted less than ten minutes and they proclaimed him guilty on all counts. After another minute or two of consultation the translator announced the verdict: "Leutnant Johann Hauser, you are hereby sentenced to serve twenty-five years of hard labor."

CHAPTER 18

J ohann didn't remember how he returned to his cell. He plummeted to the ground, curling up into a tight ball, oblivious to anything around him. The desperation about his sentence seeped into his bones, crowding out anything else.

With all hope vanished, he glimpsed one of the inscriptions on the walls, wondering if those who'd been here before had felt as utterly and completely hopeless as he did in that moment.

He would never survive twenty-five years in a camp. Not in his deteriorated physical condition. He barely weighed eighty pounds and there was no flesh or muscle anywhere to be found in his body.

An idea formed in his head, a last desperate attempt to take his fate into his own hands. For lack of a belt, he'd girded up his trousers with a rope. That rope would now serve its purpose to escape from his dreadful life. Johann gazed up at the single light bulb, gauging whether the support bracket would be strong enough to hold his body weight when he hanged himself.

The door to his cell opened even as he pondered the best way to get the rope and himself up there. Two guards walked in.

"Hands against the wall, feet spread apart."

Hadn't they searched him a dozen times already? What else did they expect to find? Johann instinctively brushed the front pocket of his shirt with Lotte's picture with his hand as he raised it to obey the command. Soon, he wouldn't need the picture anymore. He just regretted not having been able to say goodbye to his beloved girl. Would the Soviets even inform her? Or would she never find out his fate?

The hands of the guard searching him, brushed past the photograph, but stopped on his waistband. "Turn around and hold up your shirt."

Johann did as demanded and exposed his caved-in stomach and protruding ribs.

"Take off the belt."

A flicker of anger heated his heart before he untied the rope, pulled it from the trousers and handed it to the guard, who examined it with a grave expression on his face.

"We don't want you to get any ideas," the guard said and pocketed the rope.

Johann saw his hopes for a quick end dashed. He would cry if he had any tears.

"You need to appeal the decision against you to Moscow," the other guard said.

"What difference would it make?"

"Only the higher court can decide. This is a lawful country."

"I'm sure it is." Johann had enough experience with the Soviet administration to seriously doubt the lawfulness of their regime. If they insisted, he would naturally write an appeal, but he didn't expect that to change the outcome of his trial.

The appeal would probably be filed and noted on several lists, serving to cover their asses in case anyone ever questioned the trial. Appearances needed to be kept up at all costs.

The guards led him to another room, furnished with a table and a chair. One sheet of paper and a pencil lay on the table.

"Write your appeal right now."

After he finished, Johann knocked on the door and a young woman with a sympathetic smile came inside. She handed him a postcard with a Red Cross logo in the corner and said, "Write quick and I'll see that it gets sent."

What was he supposed to write? If he survived, he'd be fifty-seven by the time he returned home.

He'd always believed the end of the war would improve things, would allow him to live a happy life at last. But apparently, he was wrong. Joy no longer existed in this dismal new world, no better future, nothing but pain, sorrow and bleakness.

With little time to think, he sat on the chair and penned a message to Lotte. When he was done, he handed the postcard to the woman, not daring to look into her face, for fear she'd notice the darkness in his soul.

Twenty-five goddamn years!

CHAPTER 19

Berlin, June 1948

L otte was at the university, chatting with her girlfriends about the upcoming finals. She'd adapted surprisingly well to studying at university and diligently did her homework each night. Well, most of the nights. On Fridays, she went out with her friends to bars, dance clubs or the motion pictures.

Life was good, but it could be so much better with Johann by her side. Not a single day passed that she didn't think about him, hoping he'd return home like his friend Karsten and her own father had.

From her professor she knew that the Allies had agreed at the Moscow Conference, one year prior, to release any and all German POWs by December 1948. That was only half a year away and gave her hope to be reunited with Johann before Christmas.

Lotte smiled. She couldn't wait to see him again, lose herself in his arms and finally present him to her family. Anna and Peter were preparing to leave Germany for Harvard University in the United States, but Ursula was still living in Berlin on Gatow Airbase with Tom and their daughter Evie.

The Western Allies had returned most of their POWs, except for those who wanted to stay voluntarily in France as civil workers. And while the Soviet Union dragged their feet, they had sent home close to half a million men since the Moscow Conference. Once or twice a week a new transport arrived at the transit camp Friedland near Göttingen. But the Russians needed to up the frequency of their transports if they intended to repatriate the remaining estimated one million men before the end of the year.

She bounded up the stairs to her apartment, taking three steps at once. Unlocking the door, she took off her coat to put it on the rack in the hallway. Anna's coat hung there, indicating her sister was home. Lotte would miss her. A lot.

A worrisome thought entered her mind. With Anna, Peter and Jan gone, she would be the only occupant of the family apartment. On her own she wouldn't be able to pay the rent. A knock on the door distracted her and she opened it to see the mailwoman standing on the landing with a strangely disturbed face.

"Here, this is for you," the mailwoman handed Lotte a postcard. It had the Red Cross logo in the corner and Lotte's pulse raced in her throat.

"Thank you," she said, pressing the postcard against her

heart. Despite the mailwoman's apparent need to exchange gossip, she dismissed her and flopped on the sofa to read the postcard.

She caressed the paper, reading her name in Johann's spidery handwriting that was so different from the way it used to be before his captivity. It didn't matter. He was alive. That was all that counted.

Turning the postcard she began to read –

Dearest Lotte,

It is with a heavy heart that I must tell you that I have been sentenced to twenty-five years in a Russian prison.

Lotte didn't remember screaming, but that's exactly how Anna found her moments later. Hysterical with grief, she clutched the dreadful postcard to her heart.

"What's wrong, sweetie?"

Lotte shook her head.

"Stop screaming, please." Anna climbed beside her on the sofa, wrapping her arms around Lotte's shoulders. "Please tell me."

"Johann," Lotte whispered. That fatal sentence echoed through her mind, rendering her unable to read the rest.

Anna pried the postcard from her fingers and read it out loud –

Dearest Lotte,

It is with a heavy heart that I must tell you that I have been sentenced to twenty-five years in a Russian prison.

Please do not wait for me. Find another man you can love and build a life with him.

Know that I love you with every cell of my body. Loving you has given me the strength to survive this long. My mind will be at peace if I know you are living a happy life.

Love Forever,

Johann

"Oh, my god, Lotte. I'm so sorry," Anna held her, rocking her back and forth as she continued to scream and cry in anguish.

"Why?"

"I don't know. It might be a mistake. They may reverse the verdict..."

"You know those vile Russians. They will never..." Lotte broke out in even louder bawling.

"They may let him go after a few years..."

"A few years! Do you know how the men look when they return from Russia? How much longer can he survive this?"

"You have to have faith," Anna said.

"Faith? In what? In a God who has abandoned us? Or in the corrupt Russian legal system?" Lotte's voice echoed from the apartment walls, no doubt carrying over into the neighboring flats.

"Please, calm down, will you?"

"Why? Anyone knows the Soviet court trials are a sham! Those Stalinists are worse than Hitler was! But nobody dares raise their voices. Those bastard communists will be the ruin of all of us!"

"Lotte, please..."

"You can talk. Your man came home three years ago. And you're leaving this sorry place that's called Berlin." Lotte's voice broke down.

Anna looked at her for a long minute and then said, "Do you want to come with us to America? I'm sure Professor Scherer could arrange a visa for you."

For a short moment Lotte was tempted. It would be the perfect way out, leaving all her sorrows behind. The food shortages, the lack of heating, the buildings in rubble, everything… But she shook her head. "That's nice of you, but I can't. I have to stay and wait for him. What if he returns and I'm not here?"

"You seriously want to wait for him? Haven't you read his plea to find yourself another man?" Anna said.

Lotte pushed out her lower lip. "I know he's not serious about this. He just wants me to be happy."

"And what's so bad about him wanting you to be happy?"

"Nothing." Another wave of violent sobs wracked Lotte's body. She curled up into a ball, clinging to the notion that twenty-five years wasn't that long a time.

Finally, she got up and threw herself onto her bed.

She didn't leave her room for two full days, despite the coaxing, sweet-talking and threats of her family.

When she emerged on the third day, she told Anna, "I'm ready to live again. And I will not give up. On the contrary, I will fight for Johann's return every way possible. Even if I have to speak to Stalin himself!"

"You're not going to do anything stupid? Are you?" Anna asked with horror in her voice.

Lotte had to giggle at the sight of Anna's shocked face and said, "Don't worry. This time I will fight only with legal means. But one thing I can guarantee you: he will return. And if it takes the entire twenty-five years, I won't give up. Not until I take my last breath."

"I believe you will." Anna said. "And I so hope you're successful."

CHAPTER 20

The prison in Voronezh was only a way station. Several days after his trial ended, Johann was crammed into one of the so-called *Stolobinskiwaggons* and sent to a detention camp.

After a few days he was ordered, along with several hundred other prisoners, to a gulag, a hard labor punishment camp, in Vorkuta.

Please, God. Let this place be anywhere but Siberia.

It turned out that Vorkuta was right at the border with Siberia, west of the Ural Mountains. But that didn't mean it was a better place, because it was located several miles north of the Arctic Circle. When one of the Russian prisoners told him those details, Johann's bones turned to jelly. He wished he'd die right there and then.

A rifle butt against the back of his head made him change his mind and he trotted forward, boarding yet another train of horrors.

The Arctic Circle. He closed his eyes in desolation. *Why are you doing this to me? Why? How have I deserved this?*

In other circumstances, he might have cried. But after his violent breakdown in the prison cell, he simply didn't have any emotions left. It felt as if his soul had left his body altogether, leaving behind a barely functioning empty shell. A human body devoid of sentiments. An automaton, really.

The journey to the far north into the icy Arctic wastelands took an entire week. With each passing day, his apathy and desolation increased. He was a dead man walking. Destined to languish in a gulag until the Soviets had squeezed every last ounce of manpower from his emaciated body. He'd never see home again.

In contrast to his first transport as prisoner years ago, this time they were given food and water every day. They were even allowed to step outside to pee when the train halted. It seemed the Soviets were actually interested in seeing that the passengers reached their destination alive.

Johann wasn't sure whether this was a good sign. At times he longed for a quick release from his suffering and the next moment his will to survive stirred and he promised himself to hold on. Mostly, though, he slept through the journey. It might be the last time in years to receive sufficient sleep.

When they finally arrived at the camp in Vorkuta, he doubted his perception of reality. Certainly, he must be hallucinating it – a paradise created from his delirious mind. The vast lands were blooming in the brightest yellow and purple colors. The dark-blue sky overhead greeted him with a blinding sun burning down with surprising strength.

Had the train accidentally gone elsewhere?

But no, the entrance sign clearly said Vorkuta.

All the newcomers were put into barracks and were told they had one week to adapt to the climate and the conditions in the camp.

"Well, that's an unexpected treat," Igor, a Russian anticommunist from Johann's transport, said in almost fluent German.

Johann nodded. It was nice. The first week fooled him into believing being there wouldn't be such a horrible fate. The sun shone relentlessly, the rations were more generous than in his last camp and he had to do only light work. Unloading food, sweeping the barracks, peeling potatoes. Compared to Voronezh, this resembled paradise.

The honeymoon ended much too soon. By the beginning of week two, the newcomers were distributed to regular work details, mostly in the vast mines around Vorkuta. Johann was assigned to the coal mining detail.

"Name?" the leader of the work campaign asked him.

"Hauser," Johann said.

"Sentence?"

"Twenty-five years."

The other man laughed, baring a row of rotten teeth. "Don't worry. Nobody has to live here for twenty-five years."

"They don't?" A rush of relief swamped Johann's bones.

"No. You'll die long before that."

The sarcasm crushed him, making it hard to breathe. The work was excruciating and after he toiled ten hours loading hundredweights of coal onto train wagons with nothing but his bare hands, he only made it back to the camp with his new friend Alfred's help.

Over the course of the last week Johann had made friends with two men who couldn't be more different: the quiet and sly Igor, who was usually well informed, and a German called Alfred. Alfred was a unique specimen: a former boxer, whose body still looked the part. Despite starvation and overexploitation he hadn't lost his natural determination to seek trouble.

Any brawl in the camp, and one could be sure Alfred was in the thick of it. It was almost as if he enjoyed getting punished. Johann's initial response was to steer clear of the troublemaker, but he soon realized that even the criminal gang members in the camp respected Alfred's brute force.

Johann flopped onto his bunk like a flour sack and only opened his eyes when Igor said, "If you don't get up, someone else will eat your dinner."

Dinner? He'd all but forgotten that anything but work existed in this world. With aching bones he got up from his bunk and followed the others to the kitchen barracks for a bowl of disgusting soup and a slice of bread.

Thus passed the days in a cruel monotony of eating, sleeping, and working. Mostly working.

One day Igor said, "Did you know there's a culture barracks behind the administration building?"

"A what?" Johann stared into his bowl, a fish soup. He'd been lucky that day and had found a morsel of fish in it. It was part of a fish head, but who cared?

"It's some kind of library. We should go."

"Pshaw… reading books? I have better things to do," Alfred said.

Johann, though, was intrigued. "Do you think they have anything in German?"

"I doubt it," Igor grinned. "But your Russian is quite good."

It was, because he'd diligently practiced that skill the moment he'd found out that speaking Russian gave an invaluable advantage. It allowed him to communicate with the guards and other prisoners. Keeping exclusively to the German *plenni* was what most of his comrades did. But that proved to be a mistake, because the Germans were constantly harassed by the other nationalities.

"Maybe my speaking, but I can't read the letters."

"I'll teach you."

In the culture barracks they found several classics of Russian literature alongside Marx and Lenin. But the sight of a newspaper caused giddiness to take hold of Johann.

A real newspaper! A copy of the party paper *Pravda* meant news from the outside world. Like every prisoner he craved to know what was going on in the rest of the world. For the past years the *plenni* had been deprived of information. Hungry for news he grabbed the paper and with Igor's help deciphered the headline.

"It's too difficult. Can you read the rest to me?" he begged his friend.

Igor laughed good-naturedly. "Only if you promise to read two lines tomorrow."

"Promise."

Pravda was full of communist propaganda. But with Igor's tactful *translation* into the real meaning behind the words, Johann formed an image of the happenings in the outside world.

After several weeks he was able to read an entire article

on his own. Having a link to the real world, even though only through propaganda news, gave him hope.

As the weeks passed, so did the summer. Up there, north of the Arctic Circle, the summer lasted six weeks and the winter ten months. Johann soon learned that an Arctic winter wasn't something to look forward to.

One day, the prisoners were handed padded jackets and a *dokar*, a sheepskin worn with the woolen side against the body. They also received felt boots called *valenki* and fur caps.

This was much warmer clothing than Johann had ever possessed during his time in Voronezh during the harsh winters. It was ironic, but it seemed he'd freeze less up here in the Arctic. At least that was what he thought.

Throughout the next months, though, he was disabused of that idea. The thermometer fell steadily and reached temperatures Johann didn't believe existed.

The work in the freezing cold became harder and ever more tedious. More than one of his comrades froze his fingers, toes, or nose. It started out with burning, itching, then nothing. The exposed skin became ghostly white and turned black when the affected man didn't instantly counter the freezing by rubbing the skin with snow – a trick Johann had learned in his last camp.

In the evenings he often heard the harrowing screams of men who had their toes or fingers amputated by the imprisoned doctors without any means of anesthesia. The kindest thing a doctor could do was to knock out the patient with a punch to his head before operating.

Johann trudged on. On very cold days, he wore a *baschlyk*, a hood that was fastened at the neck and only left three small holes for eyes and mouth. While the *baschlyk* certainly helped to keep the worst cold away, it made working an agony.

Beneath the cloth, the sweat turned to ice, forming icicles around mouth and nose. Johann found it difficult to breathe the humid air, but on the other hand, breathing without the hood burned his lungs. There really was no good way to work under the extreme temperatures.

The native people did the only reasonable thing to counter the harsh conditions and rarely left their houses during winter. Like bears they hibernated, their lives reduced to the bare essentials. A luxury the *plenni* couldn't afford. They were forced to work even through the worst of the cold.

Therefore Johann was quite surprised when one day a guard announced with an important expression, "No outside work today."

"Why's that?" Alfred said. "Surely not out of the goodness of their hearts."

Despite his misery, Johann had to suppress a grin. "Surely not."

"Because it's too cold," Igor said. "Below minus thirty it's simply impossible to work outside."

"Quiet!" the guard bellowed. "Your labor detail is assigned to repair all broken bunks in the barracks."

Repair how? Johann didn't voice his concern. For now he was content with not having to go outside. Not that anyone would consider their barracks *warm*, and the *plenni* wore their padded jackets and sheepskins day and night. But at least it stayed above the freezing point inside.

The next day the guards asked for volunteers to bring

wood logs to the commandant's house. Johann wasn't keen on extra work, especially not if it involved a two-mile walk through the white hell surrounding them.

Igor took him and Alfred by the elbows and stepped forward. "We will volunteer."

"Are you crazy, you idiot?" Alfred hissed, readying his fist for a good brawl.

Johann jumped between the two men. It was too late to protest anyway. The guard had already jotted down their names on a list. Together with five other volunteers they loaded wooden logs onto a *panje* sled. Usually, a horse or a pack of huskies drew this kind of sled, but in the gulag, men replaced the animals.

Johann swore beneath his breath, promising Igor eternal wrath for signing them up for this goddamn mission. When they reached the commandant's mansion, his eyes widened with awe.

It was a real house, made of concrete, no doubt by unfortunate prisoners. The guards fled inside and left the prisoners to do the work unsupervised.

When Johann first entered the storage room to unload and stack the wood, he couldn't believe how warm it was. Combined with the hard work, the cold soon left his bones and he shed first the padded jacket and then the sheepskin. Even Alfred stopped grumbling and showed a grin on his bearded face.

After finishing their work, they settled against the stacked wood, waiting for a guard to come and tell them what to do next – though nobody was in a hurry to get going again. Simply sitting in the warmth was a joy they'd long missed. Meanwhile, the unforgiving wind had roared into a veritable snowstorm, rattling and jarring at the doors and windows.

One of the guards came to check on their progress and gave them wonderful news. "The storm's too strong. We have to stay here for the night. You are allowed to sleep in the storage room."

Igor rose to speak. "*Tovarish*, will we receive some food, please?"

It seemed the guard hadn't thought about such mundane things as food for the prisoners, because he furrowed his brow and then shrugged. "I guess you should, right?" Then he turned to leave.

Nothing happened for a long time and the only sound Johann heard was the howling wind. But then the door opened, and an old Russian woman came inside. When Johann noticed the tray she was holding in her hands he wanted to fall to his knees and kiss her feet.

"The commandant ordered me to bring you food," she said in Russian and put down the tray filled with delicacies Johann hadn't tasted in years. Looking at the men she shook her head. "You're much too skinny. I'd better get some more."

The moment she vanished, eight men attacked the food like a pack of wolves. Johann's mouth watered at the aromatic smell of a hearty stew. He sunk his spoon deep into the pot and dug out a piece of potato. Joy filled his heart as the heavenly taste and creamy substance of the stew filled his mouth, the hot liquid running down his throat and warming his stomach from within.

The stew was filled not only with potatoes, but also with chunks of meat, carrots, cabbage, and onions. It bore no similarity to the dishwatery soup they received at the camp. Within a minute the men emptied the entire pot and dug their teeth into thick slices of bread spread generously with butter – real butter.

The old woman looked quite surprised when she saw the pot emptied to a shine and not a morsel of bread left on the tray. She smiled at them and put down more food. *Kasha*, apples and sweet cakes.

"Bless you, good woman," Johann said. This time the men savored the food, basking in the feeling of being full. Sated.

"Have you heard? A bunch of German POWs have been released," Kurt said.

"We're not POWs anymore, we're convicted criminals," Johann answered. "The Russians made sure of that with their phony trials."

"But there were cases of sudden release even of those convicted to twenty-five years."

"You dream on," Alfred said. "As soon as it's summer, I'll escape."

"What?" The four Germans plus Igor jerked their heads and stared at him.

"You heard me." Alfred nodded, indicating this was his last word about the topic.

While Johann didn't believe such an undertaking had any chances of success, he admired Alfred for being so daring. Himself, he'd come to terms with the imprisonment and accepted it as an unchangeable fate. If he had to spend his life in prison he might as well make the most of it.

Naturally, he hoped that one day he'd leave the place the Russian prisoners called *Devil's Home,* but he was determined not to waste away and to enjoy his life within very limited boundaries.

Staying healthy was essential for his plan. Each day he made hot tea with Icelandic moss that he picked on his way to work. He learned to speak, read and write Russian, read the newspaper and classic literature, did gymnastics to stretch what remained of his muscles and minimize injuries, and found joy in the little things. Like sitting idly in a warm room with a full stomach.

CHAPTER 21

Summer 1949

C hristmas came and went, but everybody was too exhausted to notice. Winter passed and summer chased away the brutal cold. The prisoners planted vegetables to supplement their diet, repaired their barracks, and made small embellishments here and there.

Since the *plenni* didn't have reliable information, they lived purely on the plentiful rumors. Every other week one of the men spread the latest gossip about a general amnesty for prisoners of war, gleaned from reading between the lines of a *Pravda* article or an overheard conversation between two guards.

Sometimes miracles happened and German POWs were transferred away, either home or to another camp. The

Soviets never gave an explanation and the prisoners didn't dare ask.

Johann lived day by day, making the best out of a horrible situation. He'd become quite fluent in Russian and used his day off to read the books from the culture barracks.

In Vorkuta, every prisoner was allowed one day off per week, called *vikhodnoy*, which translated to going out. A cynical name, really, because this was the one day the prisoners didn't have to leave the camp.

Johann had long given up the notion of getting angry or even annoyed at such blatant mocking from the Soviets and instead enjoyed the leisure time. Most prisoners slept all day, but he buried his nose in books that transported him into a better world far away from the Devil's Home.

In his mind he wrote letters to his beloved Lotte, the thought of her making him sad and happy at the same time. He imagined her in all her beauty with children tugging at her hands – she deserved to be happy. But although he wished the best for her, he hated the idea of another man by her side, and in his dreams those children belonged to him.

To them.

In reality, there were no letters. The Soviets held a hysterical fear that a prisoner might write something bad about them and let the outside world know the truth. Johann scoffed; there were more than enough abominations to write about. In his opinion, the Communists were on a par with the Nazis in terms of injustice, cruelty, misanthropy and mendacity.

Like Hitler, Stalin justified even the cruelest crimes with

his flawed ideology. Johann sighed. Would humanity never learn? Hadn't the Romans killed the Christians two thousand years ago? And hadn't then the Christians killed the Muslims in the crusades a thousand years ago? Hadn't even the Christians amongst themselves fought to the last drop of blood in the Thirty Years War four hundred years ago? All to preserve a flawed ideology that decreed there was only one correct path to follow. When would humanity finally learn to leave those in peace who looked, thought, and lived differently?

Johann wouldn't hold his breath.

"Hey, what're you up to?" Alfred strolled into the library.

"As you can see, I'm reading." Johann held up the book *Anna Karenina* by Leo Tolstoy. It was tough reading and only with Igor's help had he managed to get past the first page.

"Reading, always reading. Come outside, the sun is finally shining. And I have bartered *machorka*."

"Now I know why you stuck your nose into the library," Johann said with a laugh and walked over to the basket with the *Pravda*. He tore off half a page and handed it to Alfred.

Outside, Alfred took the newspaper and rolled the Russian tobacco with surprising agility. Then he ripped the finished cigarette into two pieces and handed one to Johann.

"Ahhh… that's good." Johann savored the sweet taste. It had taken him a while to get used to the taste of *machorka*, but now he looked forward to such a treat. They usually smoked it rolled in newspaper. Not only out of necessity, but also because it simply tasted best.

Igor had explained that the newspaper publishers used a special kind of paper explicitly for this second usage. In a

Soviet Union riddled with shortages, one could not let anything go to waste, not even an old newspaper. Other second uses were less appetizing but equally appreciated.

"We should organize a football game," Alfred said, taking a deep lungful of smoke.

"Are you nuts? Who has the energy for a game?"

"It'll be fun. And we desperately need some fun." Alfred looked at the meager remains of his formerly bulky muscles. "And some practice, or before long I'll disappear completely."

"You go and do that." Johann shrugged. He took another deep inhalation of the sweet tobacco. Should Alfred organize a football game, he'd sit on the bank rooting for the teams.

About an hour later Alfred returned. "All set."

"What?" Johann looked up from his book.

"The game, idiot. Haven't you listened to me?" Alfred punched him playfully in the shoulder. "Come on."

With a deep sigh Johann closed his book. Alfred was a great friend and good companion but sometimes he was simply a pain in the ass.

The courtyard had been converted into a makeshift field, two wooden logs on each side standing in for the goal. On the field twenty-one players waited for Alfred to return. One team was comprised of the well-fed gang bosses, kitchen workers and other privileged prisoners.

But Johann's breath caught in his lungs when he saw the opposing team dressed in uniform. The guards exchanged their rifles and truncheons for a ball. The rest of the prisoners on *vikhodnoy* stood around the field waiting eagerly.

A whistle blew and the game began. For the next half an hour Johann forgot about the misery of his existence and cheered on the prisoner team. Ultimately the guards won, which was probably the wisest outcome.

Everyone, including the guards, enjoyed the small reprieve from the harsh reality and the guards showed their appreciation by doling out double rations in the evening. Alfred beamed from one ear to the other, already making plans for the next event.

CHAPTER 22

Summer slipped away much too quickly, and winter arrived. The weather turned cold and before Johann knew it, the first snow fell. Life in Vorkuta was brutal and inhumane, but he'd gotten used to it. It was what it was. There was no use in moping around over things he couldn't change.

The men who incessantly crabbed usually got punished or lost their will to survive. One could literally watch the flame of life snuff itself out in a man. From the moment the soul gave up, the body lasted a week at most.

Johann often thought about Helmut, hoping his friend had made it home safely. Helmut had been his anchor, his beacon in a thunderous sea. He smiled at the memory. Despite having been conscripted by force, Helmut had rarely complained. He'd held such an unshakable faith in his God that even the bleakest days in their captivity couldn't break his spirit.

Himself, he wasn't very religious. In his opinion the

profession of a solider and being a Christian didn't mesh well. A soldier poised to kill, whereas a Christian should not.

But he agreed with Helmut on one point: a man needed a purpose to withstand the abhorrent conditions. Those who didn't find meaning in their suffering soon succumbed to illnesses or exhaustion.

During his time before the sentence his reason had been Lotte. The prospect of returning to her had kept him alive, had made him hang on for just another day and another day… but after?

He'd been on the verge of suicide, only prevented by the meticulous body search of the Soviet guards. For a long time it had felt like a curse, but he now saw it had been a blessing in disguise. He was still alive.

After many months in Vorkuta he'd finally found his reason to survive: he would return to Germany and be witness to the injustices committed by the Soviets. He'd tell the world what happened here in the wastelands of the Arctic zone, Siberia, the Eurasian steppe, everywhere in the vast country that was the Soviet Union.

Then, the world would act and free the trapped people from the yoke, or at least remember the dead. With his newfound mission, Johann hung on to life for just another day. One day at a time.

Approximately a week before Christmas, the commandant promised the German prisoners an extra day off. The communist official glanced down at the thousands of bedraggled prisoners standing in the courtyard and said, "In order to earn your day off on Christmas, you first have to make up for the lost time."

The *plenni* groaned almost inaudibly. Of course there was a catch, there always was.

"If you overachieve your target, everyone will receive millet *kasha* and sugar broth on Christmas day."

Kurt hissed, "Sugar broth? Yummy…"

Johann's mouth watered at the image of the sugary soup running down his throat. Sweet was a taste absent from their diet and he craved sugar like a Pervitin addict craved his next methamphetamine pill.

So they toiled, two extra hours each day for one week. They bartered and everyone pitched in with a little something to celebrate Christmas. One man organized a candle, others saved up flour rations to make a cake, again others made small presents to give.

Johann giddily awaited the festivities, more enthused even than he'd been as a child. On Christmas Day at 5 a.m. the roll call sirens went off, rousing everyone from slumber. He turned around, closing his eyes in the knowledge that they'd been granted a day off today. But shortly after, he was crudely shaken by a guard, "Get up, lazybones!"

Jerking up, his eyes opened wide, "*Tovarish*, it's our *vikhodnoy* today. We worked extra hours to get the day off."

"The commandant changed his mind. Get up and go to work."

Kurt said, "See, I told you they wouldn't keep their promise. Damn Ivan."

"I'm not going," Alfred said. "I worked my quota ahead of time, so I'm going to stay in bed."

"No, you won't. Get up to work," the guard shouted.

Alfred in his matchless defiance for authority slid out of the bed and crossed his arms in front of his chest. "No."

155

Johann took a step toward his friend. "Alfred, please."

"You! Get out of my way," the guard warned Johann and then knocked his truncheon against Alfred's shoulder. Johann had barely enough time to jump aside before Alfred unleashed his ire and attacked the guard, ramming his head into the guard's lower stomach.

The other prisoners in the barracks followed the spectacle with gaping jaws, but nobody dared intervene. Of course such disrespect for the rules couldn't last long and within a minute several more guards stormed the barracks to haul Alfred away.

The entire day at work Johann feared he'd never see his friend again. In the evening when they returned to the camp, one of the prisoners told him, "Alfred's been sent to the penal block."

Johann swallowed. At least his friend wasn't dead – yet. The penal block was where they held the murderers. Vile and vicious men with whom nobody wanted to come into contact. A shiver ran down Johann's spine and for the rest of the week worry for his friend consumed him.

But one day, Alfred showed up at the culture barracks with a grin on his face. "Hey, I'm back."

"Goddamn you, I was worried sick," Johann said.

"I'm fine. It was a nice change of routine. In fact, I should start a brawl more often."

"You're certifiably insane. What did they do to you?"

"Who?" Alfred beamed like a light bulb.

"The murderers."

"Oh, them…" Alfred made a dismissive gesture. "They're good blokes."

Johann's eyes popped out. "You're pulling my leg, right?"

"No, not at all. At first, they didn't exactly welcome me to their block, but that changed after I knocked out the three baddest guys." Alfred chuckled. "After that I offered to teach them how to box and we became fast friends."

"Are the guards aware of this?" Johann barked a short laugh.

"Sure are, that's why they brought me back. Seems I'm a poor example." Alfred laughed. "Imagine that, me corrupting hardened criminals and murderers."

"You are... simply... unique." Johann shook his head. "But I'm glad you're back, I missed you."

"Whoa... don't get all sentimental on me! I wasn't even away for a week. Will you start crying like a baby when they release you and not me?" Alfred presented a tough exterior, but Johann could see that he was touched.

"We'll be released together. What do you say?"

"Nah, after that stunt, they're not gonna release me ever. I'm sure they just piled another five years atop my sentence."

"Why? Why do you keep getting into trouble? I mean, don't you want to go home?"

Alfred made a sad face. "There's no one to return to."

"You can't give up hope—"

"I don't. Haven't you yourself pestered me with the wisdom that a man needs a mission to survive this hell?"

"I have... but how does getting into trouble help?"

"Well." Albert's face took on a determined expression. "Since I won't leave this shithole alive, I've made it my mission to cause as much grief for the guards as I can. They can punish me all they want. I'll enjoy every little fight and the satisfaction it gives me to break their stupid rules. Nobody messes with Alfred Weller!"

"It's a weird mission, but if it makes you happy, my friend, I accept your decision. To each his own."

"Know what? It may sound strange but the happiest moments in my life are when I'm involved in a brawl. It's almost as if I'm a free man again, standing in the boxing ring, ready to take on my opponent."

A few days later, one of the guards sought out Alfred, whispering in hushed tones for quite a time.

"What did he want?" Johann asked.

"Made me an offer."

"An offer for what?" Johann eyed his friend suspiciously.

"More food, light work, and women."

A gasp erupted from Johann's throat. "Women?" The last woman he'd seen was the elderly housemaid in the commandant's home a year ago. He knew they had a camp for women prisoners around here somewhere but had never actually seen one of them.

"Yep."

"What do you have to do?"

"What I do best."

Johann wanted to punch his friend but given that Alfred could crush him with one hand that wasn't a particularly bright idea. "Will you tell me the whole story, or do I have to worm it out of you?"

Alfred chuckled. "I honestly have no idea how you and I became friends. You can be so naïve. They want me to entertain them with cage fights."

"Cage fights?"

"Yes. And before you start lathering me with misguided moral objections, the winner gets to live."

"Alfred! You can't be serious about this! You can't agree to this!"

"Of course I am serious. I already accepted."

"But what if you die?" Johann couldn't fathom Alfred's reckless behavior. Apart from the objectionable morals of setting out to kill another man, why would he take such a huge risk?

"Seriously? What difference does it make whether I go down in a good fight or dragging coal to the trains?" Alfred cocked his head. "Tell me the truth. Have you never thought about suicide?"

Johann swallowed hard. "I have. But…"

"This is my chance to spend my life doing what I love most, instead of toiling all day for those wretched bastards. However long I have left on this earth, I'll enjoy it to the fullest. And I won't go to bed hungry."

"I hope you won't regret this decision."

"I won't. "

Alfred was moved immediately to another barracks for the privileged prisoners. About a week later in the short time span between dinner and bedtime, the first cage fight was announced.

All the prisoners were allowed to attend. Johann went together with Igor, biting his lips nervously. He didn't want to see his friend die, but he also didn't want to miss a chance to watch him fight.

A whistle sounded and the fight began.

Alfred moved about like the pro he was and his opponent, a burly newcomer, didn't last long. Johann closed his eyes to the bloody finish, but cheered along with everyone else when the winner was announced.

"Alfred! Alfred!" the crowd chanted as the next opponent was led into the makeshift ring.

"I can't watch this. This is barbaric," Johann told Igor and turned to leave.

"You can't leave, not now. Not when we're having fun for the first time in months," Kurt interjected.

"You call this fun?" Johann said, aghast.

"Come on. Those guys deserve it. Haven't you listened to the introductions? The last one skinned three young women alive. You can't really feel sympathy for him, can you?"

Johann shrugged. All of this was so wrong. Incredibly wrong. He thought the murdering, disguised as heroic deeds, had ended with the war. Apparently not. Instead, they'd all been reduced to beasts in the brutal environment of the Gulag Vorkuta.

Later, Johann approached Alfred. "Congratulations."

Alfred grinned. "I know you don't approve of my choice, so it means a lot that you came."

"You're still my friend. And maybe I can convince you to stop." In normal times, Johann wouldn't have associated with a man like Alfred, but what was normal in his life?

"I won't stop. This is my fate."

"Whatever happened to your mission to bring grief to the guards?"

"Well, I found a better mission: to bring much needed

entertainment to my fellow prisoners and have fun doing it." Alfred stared at Johann for a long time. "And you, my friend, you need to become more like me. You're a good man, but this won't help you here. You need to dump your conscience into the snow and become brutal and unscrupulous. In hell only the bad guys prosper."

Johann shivered. His integrity and moral values were the only things the Soviets hadn't stolen from him. He wouldn't give them up, ever. "That's not my way of doing things."

"When you change your mind, let me know. I might teach you some moves," Alfred chuckled and turned away.

CHAPTER 23

January was the bleakest month, with only a few hours of daylight each day. Johann hadn't realized how much a human needed the sun until it no longer shone. Shivering had become his normal condition and like everyone else he yearned for summer to arrive.

He *celebrated* his fifth anniversary in captivity hacking away at the ice of the frozen river, shivering like aspen leaves. That goddamn icy wind cut through Johann's clothing and scorched his skin.

His fingers had turned numb hours ago, but there was no stopping or pausing. The work detail had been assigned to hack the ice away and take out the rafts. The river was the main means of transportation for both the village people and the camp, and logistics had to be kept flowing at all costs – otherwise everyone up here would soon starve or freeze to death.

Because the banks of the river were frozen, the boats unloaded the supplies onto rafts, which made towards the ice-laden shores. The prisoners pulled the rafts out of the water and across the ice, unloaded the supplies, and then sent the rafts back out.

It was backbreaking work, but at least the guards didn't bother or hurry the *plenni,* because they preferred to keep warm by the fire. From his spot, Johann saw them circulating a bottle of vodka. He enviously eyed the flickering flames of the fire, imagining a wafting of heat coming in his direction.

He often wondered whether the guards were in Vorkuta because they'd volunteered, or if this was some kind of punishment for them, too. Surely there were more coveted jobs in the Soviet Gulag system.

A horrendous crack tore through the air interrupting his train of thought. The next moment his left leg burned with excruciating intensity.

"Help! I broke through the ice!" He screamed at the top of his lungs, trying to free his trapped leg. But since he didn't have purchase, he couldn't heave himself up. He threw his upper body onto the ice, trying to crawl forward. But his leg refused to budge. "Help!"

One of the guards looked over and then shouted commands to the other prisoners. Johann's leg had meanwhile turned numb and he felt life itself slipping from his body.

Indifferent to the hauling, pulling and shoving of his comrades, he opened his eyes again when someone forced a stinging liquid down his throat. Vodka! He swallowed and spluttered, the ferocious burning all the way down to his stomach indicating he wasn't dead.

"Take the wet clothes off him," one of the guards

commanded and people started pulling at Johann's legs. He felt how they took off his felt boots and trousers and then wrapped him in a thick blanket before laying him next to the fire.

Grateful for the warmth, Johann smiled at the village woman helping him to sit up and handing him a mug of hot tea.

"Drink this," she urged him.

He tried, but his hands trembled so violently, he spilled half of the liquid. The kind woman came to his aid, holding the mug to his lips.

For the rest of the day, Johann was released from his work duties. He finished the tea, and rubbed his leg ferociously, hoping to get the circulation running again. When the congealed blood in his leg began to flow, his face took on a pain-stricken grimace. The intense prickle felt like oversized pins and needles pinching deep into the flesh.

But agony was better than frozen toes, or – God forbid – a frozen leg. One of the guards pointed out that he had to walk back to the camp on his own feet before he could see the doctor.

A few of the villagers sitting around the fire and waiting for the supplies from the rafts struck up a conversation with him.

"German?" a man who looked like a bear asked.

"Yes."

"*Wojna kaput.*" The war is over, the Russian said.

Johann nodded. Because how was he supposed to answer? *Five bloody years ago the war ended, and I'm still here unjustly imprisoned by your corrupt and degenerated Communist leaders.*

"You must be hungry." A young woman handed Johann a piece of bread.

"Don't give him anything, since he already had tea," the guard told her off.

But she didn't budge and said to the guard, "Give them food already. They're humans, too."

"That's none of your business, woman," the guard said.

Johann, though, was incredibly grateful for that display of compassion. Not all the Russians were bad. These villagers here weren't cut from the same cloth as the vile bureaucrats in Moscow presiding over phony trials.

Another old woman sidled up to him and whispered, "I hear you get soap at the camp."

He nodded. Every *plenni* received a monthly ration of soap. He'd much rather receive food, because in winter the prisoners couldn't use the soap anyway. There was no water to wash themselves or their clothes with. Only snow. The little water they made from melting snow was used to drink or cook.

"Would you have some soap to trade?" she asked probingly.

His ears perked up. "I might. What do you have to offer?"

She looked around to make sure the guards weren't following their conversation, or they would demand a cut. "Bread."

"Bread is good, but…" Johann thought for a moment. They received bread at the camp. What he really needed were vegetables. Some of his mates had already succumbed to the sailor's illness, scurvy. "…do you have onions and potatoes?"

She nodded and they arranged a barter transaction for

the next day. Soap in exchange for potatoes, onions and carrots. Then he remembered that he might not be able to work for a few days and said, "See that man over there, the skinny one in rags with the fur hat?"

The woman looked at him with a confused expression and he almost laughed out loud. All the prisoners would fit that description.

"What's your name?"

"Nadja."

"Nadja, if I'm not here tomorrow, a man called Kurt will approach you and make the exchange."

"Why are you still talking to that prisoner? Don't you have better things to do?" One of the guards lashed out at her.

"Shut up," she told him, but stood and walked away after uttering, "Kurt. Tomorrow."

CHAPTER 24

One day Johann realized two years had passed since his trial and sentencing. Twenty-three years left to go. It felt like a hundred forevers. On days like this one, hope seeped from his body in rivulets, leaving nothing but emptiness behind. His mind clogged with bleakness and despair, crowding out every memory of happier times.

If he started to forget the world he'd left behind, did that mean they'd forgotten about him, too? He worried there wouldn't be anyone left remembering him, should he ever return home. A dry sob erupted from his throat as he tried to ground himself.

The grief over losing his beloved Lotte still weighed heavily on his heart, even after such a long time. Thoughts of her had kept him going in Voronezh, but after his trial he'd been determined to let her go, not wanting to mourn what would never be.

Recently, though, he'd started dreaming about her at

night. They weren't good dreams, because every time he reached out for her, her face became blurry and faded away. He ran after her and shouted, *Wait! Lotte, wait for me!* but the faster he ran, the quicker she disappeared into the mist. Then he jolted awake with a thundering heart, and cold sweat covering his body.

He stared into the darkness, conjuring up her face with his mind. It never worked. Ever since her photograph had fallen victim to one of the frequent purges, he had started losing her – bit by agonizing bit. First, her sweet face seeped from his memory, then the sound of her voice, the smell of her hair, the feel of her soft lips on his.

The only trace of her existence was the heartache when he pronounced her name. *Charlotte. My sweet darling Lotte.* He so hoped she'd moved on and led a happy, fulfilled life. At the same time he so hated to imagine she'd moved on to lead a life without him.

"Have you written home yet?" Igor asked Johann. The prisoners were allowed one letter every three months, but foreigners had to do so on a special form, which incidentally never was available.

"Very funny."

"No, really. I just delivered my letter and saw a small stack of the foreigner forms in the culture barracks. You'd better rush before they're all gone."

Igor had barely finished his sentence by the time Johann dashed out of the barracks. Upon arriving at the library he asked the guard in charge about the form and was given the last one. He held it against his heart.

Tears pooled in his eyes and he blinked them away. Once

it was his turn to use the pen, he settled at one of the tables, suddenly unsure what to write. Would she even remember him?

Giving a deep sigh, he wrote:

Dear Lotte,

I hope this letter finds you well and that you received my last note. Things in Vorkuta are... well, cold. But I'm doing fine and don't want you or anyone else to worry about me. Please.

If it's not too much trouble, I would like to ask you to send a package to me with essentials via the Red Cross (instructions are on the back of this form). And please, tell me about your life.

I still love you with every fiber of my soul, which is the very reason why I'm urging you not to wait for me. You deserve to live a life filled with joy and happiness. Knowing how stubborn you are, I can see you pout, but do me a favor and listen to me just for once.

There's no way I'll allow you to wait for another twenty-three years. You must enjoy your life, because I cannot. Do everything with so much joy that it's enough for both of us.

Johann

~

Three months later

"Have you heard?" Kurt and Thorsten stormed into the barracks, where Johann was unraveling thread from his blanket.

"Heard what?" He barely looked up, because he needed to collect enough material to knit socks for winter.

"They're bringing an entire train wagonload of letters and packages into the camp as we speak."

Johann dropped the blanket and gathered the loose threads into his pocket. Rushing past his comrades who stood with hanging jaws, he shouted, "What are you waiting for? Let's go."

Together they jogged all the way to the culture barracks where a huge crowd of prisoners had gathered and were waiting for the gift giving. The atheist communists didn't celebrate Christmas but getting a care package was even better.

A joyous tension hung in the air that Johann had never sensed before. The drab dullness of the camp and the apathy of the prisoners had been blown away like dust in the storm. Thousands of pairs of eyes sparkled with elation, still not comprehending the miracle that was about to unfold in front of their eyes.

Some of the Russian prisoners had received letters before – carefully screened words from their families. But none of the German *plenni* had ever received so much as a single word of news from home.

And a box full of goods? Unthinkable.

Johann kneaded his fingers. He'd told Lotte to move on, but now he hoped she'd found enough fondness in her heart to send him a package… or at least a letter. A postcard, perhaps. Anything?

He waited for more than an hour while name after name was called. But not his. There was still a stack of boxes left when the guard in charge announced, "Bedtime.

Go to your barracks. We'll distribute the rest tomorrow after dinner."

Johann folded up like a pocketknife, all energy sapped from his body.

"Hey, your name could come up tomorrow," Thorsten tried to console him, holding his own box pressed tightly against his chest.

The next evening a considerably smaller number of men gathered to await the distribution of packages. Johann had all but given up hope when only one medium-sized box remained. He turned around to return to his barracks with slumped shoulders, when someone elbowed him.

"Hey, aren't you Hauser?"

He nodded.

"They called your name!"

My name? In his profound despair he hadn't heard it, but now, he turned around and rushed toward the guard. After verifying Johann's identity, the guard handed him the box. Johann recognized Lotte's handwriting on the address label and for a moment he believed to smell her scent and feel her love for him. He swallowed down the lump forming in his throat and pressed the package to his heart.

In the barracks he put the box reverently onto his bunk and traced his fingers along the smooth cardboard. It would make a great barrier against the wind when put between his shirt and jacket in winter. Or he could use it to mend the hole in his shoe... there were endless possibilities.

He untied the cord that kept the box closed and immediately wrapped it around his waist. A piece of cord was a coveted possession one had to closely guard at all times or risk it being stolen.

When he was ready to open the box, his fingers were trembling and his heart fluttering. He closed his eyes for a moment to take a deep breath before he lifted the lid. It was full to the brim with goods he hadn't seen, tasted, or smelled in years.

Two pairs of woolen socks. The softest undershirt hand-knitted from angora wool. Worker's gloves made from sturdy canvas. His fingers carefully took out the robust dark yellow gloves and tried them on. A sigh of utter content escaped him, because wearing the gloves made the next work shift seem like a piece of cake.

But there was even more in the box. He found durable brown bread, a salami the size of his forearm, slightly shriveled carrots, lentils, chocolate and a pound of sugar carefully stacked. He couldn't believe his good luck. Sugar was as valuable a commodity as gold in the camp and an excellent bartering currency.

Only when he was done sifting through the goods did he pick up Lotte's letter. A photograph of her fluttered out. Her smile lit up her face and instantly he remembered the sound of her laughter. He traced his finger down the picture, caressing her rounded cheeks, her stubby nose and her wonderful, fiery red curls.

For a moment he was surprised, because she looked much older than he remembered her. Then he gave a snort; time for her had passed, too. *She must be...* He had to calculate her age. *Twenty-four!*

How much she must have changed from the eighteen-year-old girl he once knew to the woman she must have become. The thought stabbed at his heart. He pocketed the photograph and lifted the letter to his nose, inhaling deeply, memories of her scent rushing back to him as the smell of roses and a hint of spice reached deep into his heart and ignited a fire in his soul.

Her handwriting was generous, swinging, like the upbeat girl she was. But the line through the "t" was so strong and powerful, it made the entire word somehow belligerent, poised to attack whatever stood in her way.

He smiled. That was his Lotte. Always out to fight whatever she believed unjust. *She's not your girl anymore*, he reminded himself.

With bated breath he mustered the courage to unfold the letter, smoothing out the creases before he began to read –

Dearest Johann,

I received your postcard two years ago. It made me cry. I cried for two full days. First I cried out of sadness and grief, then out of rage. Don't you dare tell me to forget you! This is not how it works.

Without you, I wouldn't be alive today, remember that? So, even if I didn't love you with all my heart, I would still wait for you to return to my side.

So stop telling me to forget all about you, because it's an incredibly selfish, inconsiderate and cold-hearted thing to say. I'll forgive you this time, because I know the sentence must have been disturbing for you, but you'd better not mention this topic ever again! Are we clear on that?

He couldn't stop the tears rolling down his cheeks. That was his Lotte, in the flesh. Only she could scold a man imprisoned in the hell of the Arctic Zone for telling her to move on.

But his tears were happy ones. Knowing she still loved him caused a flood of joy to sweep his body. It was enough to forget his dire condition for a short while, enough even to hope for an early release. He furtively glanced around and wiped the tears away. Nobody needed to know about his emotional turmoil.

Now that the Soviets have allowed letters and packages, I will send you one every three months. If you can, write back to me and tell me what you need most.

I do have some idea, because – and you will hate this – I've been in contact with several of your friends and grilled them about every little detail that can help to make your life easier.

Again, he paused reading. Memories of Karsten stormed him. The man had been a good friend, back in his first months in Voronezh. He wondered whether one of the friends Lotte mentioned was Helmut. With every fiber of his soul he hoped Helmut had made it back home.

Lotte's letter continued with mundane facts about her life, her family, her recent trip to America to visit her sister Anna, and her graduation. She was a lawyer now and had started to work for a well-known law firm in Berlin.

Again, feelings of inferiority crept into his heart. For the rest of the world, including Lotte, life had moved on, while he was captured in an infinite loop of wretchedness. Absolute, pure, unadulterated misery.

He was a nobody, not even considered a human being, for he had none of the rights other humans possessed. He'd been reduced to a means of production. According to Marxist theory he and his fellow prisoners were nothing more than the abstract mass of labor exploited for the good of the people. Because they did not form part of the *people*.

The ever-present hatred for the Soviets and their wicked, corrupted interpretation of communism swept over him, tightening his stomach. He spat out, muttering a curse, determined to survive the unjust sentence, simply to show them that he was still a person.

He kept on reading Lotte's letter, four pages of tiny handwriting that was sometimes hard to decipher, and at the end of it, he felt almost as if he were together with Lotte in Berlin, anxiously awaiting her upcoming move to Bonn, the new capital of the Western part of Germany. Memorizing her new address, he paused again to think.

Johann had become quite adept at reading between the lines of *Pravda*, and Lotte's letter confirmed his suspicions. The Soviet-controlled Eastern part of Germany, the GDR, wasn't the worker's and farmer's paradise it was painted out to be.

It seemed that everyone, except for the staunchest supporters of communism, was looking for a way to *rübermachen*, to leave the East for a better future in the capitalist-controlled FRG. Nobody but the Soviet administration believed that *Capitalism* was an insult.

"Bedtime!" someone shouted, and Johann quickly finished the letter, before crawling under his scratchy blanket.

There are constant diplomatic talks about returning all the prisoners of war, even convicted ones like you. So, keep your chin up!

I'll do whatever is in my power to ammeliorate your life over there, and never forget that I love you with every cell of my body and every fiber of my soul. I will not – I repeat: I will not – move on! The day you return to Germany, I will be there to wrap you

into my arms.
   With love and gratitude,
   Lotte

He folded her letter and put it next to his heart, and for the first time in years he fell asleep with a smile on his face.

CHAPTER 25

Another year passed. Johann had resigned himself to his life north of the Arctic Circle. Nutrition had improved since his arrival, especially due to the care packages the prisoners were now allowed to receive.

In-demand things from Western Germany like shampoo, chocolate, or oranges could be traded very profitably with the townsfolk.

Some of the barracks had arranged for their own patch of vegetable garden, spending countless hours raking, sowing, watering, and weeding during the short arctic summer. The men took turns hauling water from the nearby river on their walk home from work.

Today was Johann's day off and together with two fellow prisoners it was his turn to watch over the potato plants. It was a boring thing to do, but with the promise of potatoes to add to his soup during the long winter ahead, he didn't complain.

Johann actually enjoyed the watch duty, except for the

inevitable scuffle with would-be thieves from other barracks, sneaking up to the vegetable patch alone or in groups, trying to steal the produce.

He was sitting in the sun when Kurt brought a piece of cardboard painted on both sides. "Wanna play a game?"

"Sure? Nine men's morris or checkers?" The men had collected light and dark pebbles to use as pieces. Another group of prisoners, who worked felling trees, had brought home scraps of wood and carved them into chessmen. Unfortunately, only half of the men were done, and Johann hoped they could complete the set before winter set in.

"Let's start with checkers. I'm white," Kurt said.

"Fine with me," Johann said, when a chilly breeze made him shiver. "Winter is coming."

"Still several weeks until it starts snowing."

"Yes, but do you think we should harvest the potatoes already?" The tubers had grown into two-foot-tall plants with an abundance of dark green leaves. His hands itched to dig up the ground and have a look.

"No way. The townsfolk have cautioned us to wait until the leaves turn brown."

"But what if the plants freeze?" Johann's gut twisted at the thought of the hard labor going to waste.

"It doesn't matter. The potatoes are protected in the earth and the moment we have the first night frost, we can dig them up."

Johann sighed. The nearer the time of harvest came, the bolder the attempts of other prisoners to steal the potatoes. Since they were locked into the barracks at night, they had installed an alarm system with tripwires and tin cans.

It had gone off twice already. So far, the perpetrator had

always escaped empty-handed, but it was only a matter of time until someone was successful.

"We might have to bribe the guards into letting us put a watch post on the patch," Johann said.

"That'll be expensive," Heinz answered.

"I know… but do you want to lose our harvest?"

"Of course not, we'll have to ask the others over dinner. Maybe someone has an idea."

Deep in the arctic winter a sudden busyness broke out at the Vorkuta camp. For some reason nobody cared to explain, Johann was one of several hundred prisoners transferred to another camp.

They were marched off in such a hurry that Johann didn't have time to say goodbye to his friends Alfred and Igor. He left a note on Igor's bunk, wishing him the best of luck, but he couldn't get to the other side of the camp to find Alfred.

The boxer had become a celebrity in the camp and seemed to enjoy his prison life as much as possible. Johann didn't hold a grudge against the man, even though he'd never condone Alfred's decision.

In many hours of talking about philosophy, religion and the core of humanity with Igor, he'd come to the conclusion that choice was what mattered most. Choice equaled freedom. Freedom was not only a human right, but also the one thing everyone yearned to possess. During his entire adulthood he had not once encountered a man or woman who didn't want to live in freedom.

Even the staunchest Nazis, the ones who advocated the oppression of entire nations, naturally wanted freedom for themselves. The *plenni* lived for the tiniest liberty granted, such as leisure time after dinner. One hour per day when they could do what they wanted – within the limits of the camp – instead of following orders.

Choice. Be one's own master. Make one's own decisions. The physical hardships aside, he and his fellows missed that most. It was dreadful to have other people decide what or when he was allowed to eat, drink, work, do, sleep or speak.

Hell, they even tried to regulate his private thoughts. The only thing the despicable Soviets hadn't regulated yet were his bodily functions, but he had no doubt they'd do so if they found it useful to get inside his body.

"Stop dreaming." Kurt elbowed him and Johann noticed that the column of prisoners was moving toward the gate of the camp.

A ferocious shiver ran down his spine. He'd hated the camp in Vorkuta with all his heart, but now that he would walk through its gate for the last time, he felt nostalgic.

Who knew what lay ahead? It could be worse – although Johann's imagination wasn't vivid enough to come up with a worse scenario than the one he was leaving behind. He shrugged, deciding to take each moment one at a time. He didn't have a choice anyway, since other people made the decisions for him.

The men boarded train wagons and for the next ten days they rattled southward through the Russian countryside. With every passing day the grim cold decreased and when the journey finally ended, the temperature hovered above freezing.

"Where are we?" Johann asked, rubbing his eyes and shielding them against the blinding sunlight.

"No idea."

"At least it's warm." Under normal circumstances Johann wouldn't have considered temperatures around the freezing point warm, but compared to the deep-freeze in Vorkuta, it felt like summer.

They soon found out they'd crossed the Soviet Union from north to south and had landed in Kazakhstan. The camp was like any other camp he'd seen so far: ugly, desolate, drab and dirty. But much to Johann's delight, the men living here looked much healthier than in Vorkuta.

Johann staked his claim on a bottom bunk right next to Kurt. "What kind of work do you think they'll have us doing this time?"

"No idea."

"Railway tracks," one of the resident prisoners said.

"What?"

"There's only one kind of work in this godforsaken place and that's making steel railroad tracks. I'm Martin, by the way." Martin extended his hand.

Johann and the other newcomers introduced themselves and Martin cast them a scrutinizing glance. "You look pretty bad, even for *plenni*. Where have you come from?"

"The Devil's Home," Johann said.

"What?"

"A place called Vorkuta north of the Arctic Circle. A gulag where all the atrocious criminals and the German *plenni* with twenty-five-year sentences are sent."

"Oh." Martin seemed uncertain whether to believe the explanation or not. "Anyhow, this place is the nicest camp

I've been to. The Kazakhs are laid-back people and they hate Moscow almost as much as we do."

"Sounds promising," Kurt said.

"You'll find out in the morning."

The next day, Johann and the other men walked out of the prison camp and three blocks down to the rail-making factory. He didn't expect much and was surprised when he was given gloves and a helmet before manning his assigned workstation.

Apparently, the Kazakhs were determined to treat the POWs like actual human beings. The work was still tedious, awful and back-breaking. Eight hours a day he manned the tempering station. Superheated liquid metal poured into earthen molds, where it cooled enough to be handled. His job was to remove the heavy tracks together with a comrade and heave them over to another workstation, where the tracks were stamped and stacked onto flat rail cars for transport to other areas of the Soviet Union.

The factory reminded him of the Nazi slogan *Räder müssen rollen für den Sieg*. Wheels have to roll for victory. Nowadays, wheels had to roll for the good of the Soviet nation on railroads built by German slaves.

Martin hadn't overpromised. Life in the camp near Almaty was a breeze compared to Vorkuta or even to Voronezh. As long as the prisoners showed up for work on time and fulfilled their quota, they were very much left alone the rest of the day.

Johann couldn't believe his own eyes when he discovered the barracks weren't locked at night and everyone was allowed to move freely about the camp at all times. They earned a tiny wage for their labor that could be spent in the village for extra food and amenities.

Some of the resident prisoners had the privilege of walking to the village unsupervised. Johann smiled. It almost felt like being a free man again. A man of choices.

"Why don't they lock us up? Aren't they afraid we'll escape?" he asked one day.

Martin scoffed. "Escape? Have you had a look around? We're in an isolated place with deadly swamps on all sides."

"Hasn't anyone ever tried?" Johann asked. Chances of a successful flight had been considerably lower in Vorkuta, but that hadn't hindered the Soviets from putting up barbed wire fences, guards with rifles, and other means of security.

"A few did. They all died in agony, if they weren't found first – and beaten to a pulp."

Having left behind the arctic wastelands he was grateful for every little betterment in his life. Food had been his main issue for the past six years; now he could eat until he was full. It still wasn't sufficient to grow fat, but at least his body recovered from the years of ruthless exploitation, and by the end of the first year in Kazakhstan he'd put on twenty pounds of pure muscle.

The only drop of bitterness coloring his contentment was that he didn't receive news from Lotte. He'd been allowed to send her a postcard, but so far, no answer. Instead of dwelling on what he couldn't have, Johann began to look around him and enjoy what he could.

The fabrication plant employed not only prisoners but many of the townsfolk as well. After months of working side by side, the villagers, and especially the women, couldn't hold their curiosity at bay and started asking question after question. *Where do you come from? What does it look like? How is life over there? Do you have a wife? And children?*

Some would even go as far as to flirt with the *plenni* and soon enough clandestine relationships formed between the Kazakh women and the German men. Even some children resulted from these secret affairs.

While Johann appreciated the beauty of the women, his heart remained with Lotte. Smiling, he remembered her letter, her pert words giving him a piece of her mind. It had been rational to set her free from the promises made, but since she refused to move on, he'd happily cling to the silver lining her unwavering love presented.

Kurt rushed into the barracks, a nervous gleam on his scrubbed and shaven face. "How do I look?"

"Like a scarecrow," Johann said, oblivious to his friend's emotional turmoil.

Kurt's face fell. "Really? I thought…"

"You look just fine," Martin said, sending a scathing stare in Johann's direction.

Johann didn't get what the fuss was all about. Since when did a man in the camp care about his looks? Normally, they were happy to be alive, not hungry, and dressed in clothes instead of rags.

"I haven't been with a woman in…" Kurt scratched his shaved chin and counted on his fingers, "…seven years."

"How on earth?" Johann's eyes almost popped out. Not because of the time span mentioned, but because it dawned on him that Kurt was set to end the drought tonight.

Kurt grinned like a fool. "Katinka and I are going out tonight and I'm pretty sure she'll let me bang her."

"Just be back before curfew, or you'll get us all into hot water," Martin warned him.

"No need to worry. If he even still knows how to do it after such a long time, he'll shoot off within seconds," another prisoner chuckled.

Kurt cast him a dark stare and the man raised his hands with a dirty grin. "What? I know what I'm talking about."

CHAPTER 26

March 1953

News of Stalin's death reached the camp and a sigh of relief surged among the prisoners. In the following weeks countless Soviet forced laborers received an amnesty and were sent home.

"Do you think they'll amnesty us too?" Johann asked.

"Who knows? They've promised as much for years, but never once kept their word," Martin answered.

"But, today at work, the Kazakh people whispered *Skoro domoi*, every time they saw me," Kurt said.

"And you honestly think some civil workers whispering *going home soon* is proof that these red bastards will actually do it this time? I have stopped counting the times they've crushed my hopes. I'm not believing any part of this, not until I'm sitting on a train westward," Martin said.

In theory, Johann agreed with Martin. It was better not to get hopes up, just to be disappointed again. On the other hand, he could see the writing on the wall, that this time it might be true.

Thoughts of Lotte invaded his heart and he sat down to write a letter to her – of course, carefully worded to not leave a single phrase open to interpretation as criticism of the Soviet system. It was quite funny, actually. Since care packages were allowed and reached the camp mostly without losses, the *plenni* led better lives than many of the locals.

The civil workers in the rail tracks factory had nick-named the camp *kapitaliza*, for the abundance of food and other amenities the prisoners received from back home. The *plenni* didn't even need to work extra time anymore in exchange for a slice of dark Russian bread or a bowl of soup.

On the contrary, the local women suddenly saw attractive men in the German prisoners: men who were better dressed, better nourished and apparently kinder to the hardworking women than their Soviet counterparts.

The camp doctor, a prisoner himself, almost went out of business with the appearance of regular care packages; and in the previous two years less than a dozen prisoners had died, mostly in work accidents, whereas in the first years after the war, several dozen died on a daily basis.

Life could have been good, if it weren't for the omnipresent nostalgia and the fact that they weren't free men. Johann's fate could change any moment on the whim of a bureaucrat who'd send him back to Vorkuta or another camp in the wastelands of Siberia. Hell on earth was always just a step away.

About a week later, important visitors graced the camp with their presence. Laurenti Beria the new Minister of the Interior and head of the Soviet secret service, sent his commissars to interrogate the remaining German prisoners of war.

Johann had a queasy feeling in his stomach when he was called to the interrogation office. The last time, many years ago, they'd fabricated thinly veiled lies from his words and used them to sentence him to twenty-five years of forced labor. Those political commissars couldn't be trusted.

Deep in his heart Johann hoped the rumors were true and the visitors from Moscow had come to Kazakhstan to prepare the release of all the *plenni*, but one could never be sure. So he didn't allow himself to get his hopes up and was determined to watch closely every single word he uttered during the interrogation.

"Good morning, can you please state your name and rank?" the commissar said in passable German. Johann was fluent in Russian, but he preferred not to disclose this fact.

"Johann Hauser, Leutnant."

After some apparently random chitchat, the commissar asked the first loaded question: "What will you tell about the Soviet Union once you return to West Germany?"

Johann was alert and had anticipated such questioning. He put his answer into careful words: "I will cast off my time in prison like dirty clothing and never once think back."

The commissar continued to poke. "Will you say that your conviction was unjust?"

Johann scratched his chin. He wanted to scream out. *Of course it was unjust. Your whole phony trial was a made-up farce and I have every right to tell the world about your inhuman system.* But he knew that those words would send him back to Vorkuta faster than he could blink.

He opened his mouth and said, "I believe that the committee on my trial stuck to the rules and laws of the Soviet Union, giving me due process."

"So, you agree with your conviction?" The commissar seemed surprised.

Careful, that's another trick question. "I'm sure you're aware that I was given the opportunity to appeal the sentence. But the higher court in Moscow refused my appeal."

The commissar made a note and then asked, "Will you go to the Americans and criticize us?"

Johann shook his head. At least this question he could answer truthfully. "I don't know any Americans and I certainly don't plan to talk with any one of them about my time as a prisoner of war."

A few more questions about the general conditions in the camp, as well as Johann's opinion about communism and fascism followed. Just when Johann began to relax, the commissar asked, "Will you invade the Soviet Union again, when given a weapon?"

In the first moment, Johann thought the commissar was joking. But no, the man's expression was serious. "Definitely not. I've had enough of war for the rest of my life and I certainly never want to experience this again."

"Well, that's all for now. Thank you."

Johann got up and stumbled out of the interrogation

room, unable to assess whether his answers had satisfied the commissar or not.

"How did it go?" Kurt asked him upon his return to the barracks.

"Honestly, I don't know."

"What do you mean?"

"They're asking all these loaded questions and I believe I dodged the lurking landmines, but who knows?"

"Oh my!" Kurt said, suddenly nostalgic. "I really, really want to return home, but I'm gonna miss Katinka."

He shouldn't have worried, because in June 1953 the people in East Germany staged a violent uprising against their Soviet-installed government. Soviet tanks suppressed the uprising two weeks later, but it had already wreaked havoc on the *plenni* in the camps east of the Ural Mountains. Release preparations came to a halt.

"As much as I admire their guts in going up against the Soviet occupiers, they couldn't have chosen worse timing," Martin complained.

"You can be sure the Russians won't release a single man after what happened," Johann added. The mission of the day was to discourage further revolts in the many occupied *brother* nations of the new Soviet empire. The fascist government had to be worshipped as the best innovation of mankind since the wheel – by believers and critics alike. Since the *plenni* understandably leaned toward being critics of the system, they had to be kept under lock and key.

"Another hope down the drain," Martin said.

Told you not to get your hopes up. Johann was too depressed to voice the thought lingering in the room. He shouldn't be surprised that the Soviets had betrayed them once again.

Over the next days, more news came in. Beria, the man behind the release plans, was arrested. The mood in the camp reached a new low point and the *plenni* stopped caring about anything at all.

Including work. Their souls heavy with shattered hopes, they worked only the bare minimum to reach the quota. It wasn't a coordinated action, or any kind of slowdown strike, it was simply the certainty that nothing would ever change, and they were cursed to spend the rest of their lives as slaves, never to see their homes and families again.

Johann often wondered if this limbo was better than the hell in Vorkuta. Because right now he believed that even if he survived the twenty-five years of his sentence, the Russians would find another phony reason not to let him go.

For a few weeks he fell into a depression deeper than the one after his conviction. How much was life worth when you were stripped of your freedom and all hope of ever regaining it?

Four weeks later the tide turned again, and the camp commander announced that release preparations had been resumed.

"I don't believe a single word he says," Johann uttered and most everyone agreed. And unfortunately, he was right. Ten thousand German prisoners were sent home in 1953, but none from the camp near Almaty.

Pravda celebrated the generosity of the Soviet government in returning ten thousand convicted war criminals.

Johann had a fit of rage and pummeled his fist against the concrete wall until he was delirious with pain.

"Whatever happened to you?" the camp doctor asked, dressing the wounds.

"Nothing," Johann pressed out between thinned lips.

"Doesn't look like nothing to me."

Johann rarely ranted about the Soviet system, because one was never truly safe from prying ears. But the doctor had proven his allegiances many times, and nobody else was in the room. "Louts! Nothing but lies! Lies, broken promises and cruel misanthropy!"

"Now I get it," the doctor said. "I'm afraid the knuckles are broken, but we need a good excuse if I'm to write you up as unable to work."

"Pah. You know what they say?"

"You really shouldn't read *Pravda*, it's not good for your mental health," the doctor joked.

"A delegation of the East German people has negotiated with Moscow, and since there's so much goodwill between the two brother countries…" Johann spat it out. "Are we talking about the same good people who protested against the Soviet oppressors and were mowed down with brutal force?"

"Shush… you don't want to be transferred to Siberia."

"I came from Vorkuta. Siberia doesn't scare me," Johann said boastfully, but deep down he was afraid. Despite everything, his life in Kazakhstan was supportable.

The doctor didn't acknowledge Johann's remark and said, "I'll write in the report that your hand got caught beneath one of the rail tracks."

CHAPTER 27

Two years later

J ohann sat in the barracks listening to a music program on the radio. About a year earlier the two engineers in the barracks had pieced together a radio from parts organized at the factory or bartered with the townsfolk.

The program was interrupted by the hourly news report nobody listened to. But something caught Johann's attention and he shouted, "Quiet!" What he heard sent his heart pounding like a jackhammer.

"What has you launching like a rocket?" someone asked.

"Lads, you won't believe it, but as we speak, the German Chancellor Konrad Adenauer is making a personal visit to Moscow," Johann answered.

"What's he want there? Curry favors with the Russians?"

"They say it's to establish diplomatic relations," Johann said.

"Diplomatic relations? What about they let us go first?"

"From what I gleaned from this news report; that's exactly what Adenauer offered. Diplomatic relations in exchange for the release of all POWs and abducted civilians still in the Soviet Union."

A hissing went through the barracks, despite Martin's warning. "We can't get our hopes up. Remember what happened two years ago." But nobody wanted to listen to him.

"What else did the reporter say?" Kurt asked.

"Nothing." During the following five days of Adenauer's visit in Moscow, the *plenni* were glued to the radio, taking turns listening to every news report they could get ahold of and translating it for those who didn't speak Russian. They scoured *Pravda* for hidden meanings in the articles and even engaged the political officer at the factory in a conversation about Adenauer's visit and the possible implications for them.

Johann and the others spent five days in an emotional whirlpool. Hope alternated with disappointment, relief with tension. The negotiations seemed stuck and nothing moved forward. Establishing diplomatic relations with the Soviet Union would mean relinquishing the sole right of representation of Germany, effectively cementing the separation of Germany into two nations. It was a bitter pill to swallow.

The final event of the state visit was a ballet performance in the renowned Bolshoi Theatre. Very befittingly, the Soviets had chosen Prokofieff's version of Shakespeare's drama *Romeo and Juliet*. The ending scene featured the handshake of the hostile Counts Montague and Capulet over the graves of their children. After the applause for the ballet dancers ended, Nikolai Bulganin and Konrad Adenauer publicly repeated the handshake for the entire world to witness.

The next day it was official. The camp commandant announced that as of now, the prisoners were free men to do as they pleased and preparations for the return of all 9626 registered prisoners of war that remained in the Soviet Union would start immediately.

"*Heimkehr!*" The shout rang out across the camp and could probably be heard across all of Kazakhstan. "We go home! Home!"

One week later, Johann and his fellow prisoners boarded a train to Germany.

"Can you believe it?" Kurt asked as he leaned back against the wooden seat.

"Not yet. I'm still waiting for them to stop the train and say it was all a mistake." Johann had been a hairsbreadth away from release more times than he cared to remember and every cell in his body stayed strung tight, waiting for disaster to strike.

"You need to have faith," Martin said. "This time it's for real."

"Maybe." Johann shivered as he relived the brutal experience of previous train rides. He felt a sudden urge to vomit at the phantom stink of feces. The maddening thirst overtook him, making him want to scream with pain. Deep-rooted memories of raw, unabated hunger. Men dying all around him and the rotting corpses emitting the most disgusting stench.

He shook his head to dispel the memories. This time, the journey was different. The *plenni* had received clean clothes, and they traveled in passenger trains instead of the dreadful cattle cars. They were free to walk around. Once a day the train stopped to load food and water for the passengers.

He should be grateful, and he was, but while the train continued its westward journey, Johann's soul wept for the men left behind – the ones he'd known and the many nameless men, thrown off the trains, hastily buried in the loamy Russian soil, worked to death, starved, succumbing to illness and cold.

Johann and the other late returnees knew they were the last sorry batch of men, ten thousand who'd survived an endless ordeal. So many had died in captivity. One and a half million. He mourned for each and every one of them, hoping they'd found peace on the other side.

The train stopped in Brest-Litowsk, the border town between the Soviet Union and Poland. Because of the change of the gauge, the ex-*plenni* changed trains.

When Johann stepped onto the platform, he was once again transported back in time. Approximately ten years earlier he'd been in the same place, headed eastward. It seemed like a lifetime ago.

A sudden fear permeated his body. What was Germany like? He'd last been in his hometown, Munich, during the war when it had been bombed to ruins. How did the people live? What did they do in their leisure time?

And… would Lotte still love him when she saw him

again? She had sent him photos of herself over the years, but he hadn't been able to do the same. What if she only loved the handsome young man he'd been ten years ago and not the broken forty-year-old ex-prisoner he was now?

In his surging panic he toyed with the idea of running away and staying in the country that had become his fate. But Kurt's voice grounded him in reality once again: "Hey, man, what do you think I should say?"

"Say to what?" Johann shrugged off the disturbing thoughts and focused on his friend.

"They're giving us the choice to go to East Germany or West Germany."

For Johann the choice was clear. Lotte lived in Bonn, so he'd go to the West. "Isn't your family in the Soviet zone?"

"My parents are…" Kurt looked quite miserable. "But I don't really want to stay under the red thumb."

"Then don't." Johann could understand his friend's feelings. Being in East Germany didn't make one truly free from Soviet despotism. In the camps he'd often met men from the so-called communist brother countries who had been convicted in a trial equally as phony as Johann's own.

"But how?

"Simply tell them your relatives live in the West, let's say in… Bonn." Johann suggested. "I don't think they are able to find out whether that's the truth or not."

Kurt seemed uncertain but nodded.

"Look at it this way: the Russians have been lying to us for ten years, now you return the favor and lie once to secure a better life for yourself."

The train whistled and the men hurried to board the wagons. Nobody wanted to be left behind, not so close to freedom. During the journey traversing Poland, men in the bluish-green uniform of the *Volkspolizei*, the East German people's police, entered the compartments and started to ask the ex-*plenni* whether they wanted to get off in East Germany or travel on to West Germany.

Very few wanted to stay in the East, which obviously didn't please the policemen.

One of them handed out black-and-white photographs of emaciated women dressed in rags, holding dirty children by their hands. "This is what the West looks like."

Johann squinted his eyes. He had no doubt the picture was real, but from Lotte's descriptions in her letters things had changed considerably in the past five years. When given the choice to believe her or the *Vopos*, the decision was easy.

"And this…" The *Vopo* handed out newspaper articles of clean, well-fed and well-dressed children with large cornets of colorful cardboard in their hands on their first day of school. Another picture showed athletes competing in several disciplines during the GDR championships. All the pictures gave the impression of happy people in a happy nation. "…is the Democratic Republic of Germany."

"Why would you want to go to the imperialist West if you have the chance to live in the happy democratic East?" the other *Vopo* asked.

Johann decided to indulge them. "It sounds tempting. But first I have to go and find my girl in Bonn. Then I'll tell her everything you told me and I'm sure she'll want us to move to the GDR."

The *Vopo* stared at him, slightly shaking his head. "No need, there's only one chance for you to accept our generous offer and that's now."

The policeman's words confirmed Johann's suspicions and he politely declined. He hadn't actually needed this confirmation to make up his mind, because he'd seen the contents of the care packages coming from the East and compared them to those coming from the West. It was pretty clear where he wanted to go. Even if it weren't for the economic advantages, and for Lotte, he still wouldn't want to stay under Soviet rule. Every single minute in their sphere of influence was one minute too long.

Rattling wheels lulled him into sleep as the train crossed Poland and finally stopped at the border to East Germany in Frankfurt an der Oder. Johann woke with a start as everyone was ushered from the train.

Fear rushed up his spine when he saw the same policemen from the train chatting up their colleagues waiting on the platform. But the moment of panic passed when he was sent to join an ever-increasing crowd of men, waiting for another train to take them to the West.

Very few men had decided to stay and were marched off into a welcome camp, from where they'd be distributed to their final destinations in the Soviet zone of Germany. Johann didn't envy those men. They had chosen this place not because they valued the generous offer, but to be reunited with their families.

He hoped things weren't as bad as the rumors indicated. Certainly, they had to be a million times better than in the Soviet camps.

After two days' wait, the journey continued. They passed through Berlin – the former capital of Germany – Leipzig, Weimar, Erfurt, Eisenach and then reached the zonal border between the two Germanys in Herleshausen.

The train stopped and men in green uniforms peeked inside. "*Bundesgrenzschutz.*"

"West German border police?" Johann asked, suppressing the slight tremble in his voice.

"We sure are, and happy to welcome you home," the policeman said with a broad grin. "Please get off the train."

Everyone disembarked and walked the hundred yards to the inner German border. The entire time, Johann's anxiety plucked at his insides, screaming that something would go wrong in the last minute.

But the moment he passed the white turnstile, all the tension fell finally off his shoulders and he felt free.

Free!

In a sudden outburst of emotion, he followed the example of others and knelt down to kiss the native soil.

After ten and a half horrific years he had returned home.

CHAPTER 28

Bonn, September 1955

L otte waited at the airport for Chancellor Adenauer's return from Moscow. The announced press conference had drawn thousands of visitors, eager to hear the official announcement about the fate of the German prisoners of war.

For her, though, it wasn't an abstract wish for the missing men to return home. She wanted Johann. Ten years had passed and not a day went by that she didn't miss him. On the surface, she was a modern, successful and happy woman. She worked as a lawyer, earned enough money to afford a nice apartment and fancy clothes and had saved up enough to buy a VW Beetle earlier that year.

Only one ingredient was missing for her to be completely happy: her man. Her friends and family had long ago given up trying to pair her off with eligible bachelors, for she stubbornly remained loyal to Johann.

Month after month she sent him letters and care packages, always hoping that he survived whatever the Soviets threw at him. That he'd one day return to her side.

A murmur rumbled through the crowd, "He's coming."

Moments later the Chancellor appeared with his entourage and spoke into the microphones. He announced that the Soviet Union had agreed to return the last ten thousand remaining POWs.

"He'll come home," Lotte whispered, completely overwhelmed by her emotions. Her eyes filled with tears and she barely noticed the scene unfolding in front of the crowd.

"Who's that?" someone asked.

Lotte looked up and saw an old woman, dressed in a black coat and black hat, approach Adenauer. She took his hand and sank onto her knees in front of him.

"What's she doing?" someone murmured.

The Chancellor, who was about the same age as the old woman, helped her up, but she refused and kissed his hands instead. The entire scene lasted only for a few seconds, but it made a lasting impression not only on everyone present, but also on those who saw it on television.

Lotte herself could only stare at the back of the retreating woman. She knew exactly what the other woman felt. Gratitude. Joy. Elation. Tears rolled down her face as her own emotions overwhelmed her.

A few weeks later the arrival of the first transports of former POWs was announced. Lotte asked her boss for leave and the next morning she and her trusted Beetle were on the Autobahn to the release camp in Friedland.

Nobody knew who would arrive when, but she didn't care. She'd be there every single time a transport arrived until she found Johann.

She'd waited ten years; a few more weeks didn't scare her.

CHAPTER 29

Johann boarded a bus that would bring him to the *Entlassungslager Friedland.* Now that he truly and irrevocably was out of danger, his limbs began to shake.

The fifty-mile trip from the border to the camp was lined with tens of thousands waving of and smiling people. Every time the bus passed through a village, it had to slow down, because people jumped the vehicle to throw flowers through the windows and sneak a peek at the returned prisoners. Women held onto the windowpanes, intent on touching the hand of one of the men inside.

Johann's eyes widened more with every minute. What happened here had been beyond his wildest imaginings. Apparently half of the Germans were up on their feet to celebrate – him. Suddenly he didn't feel like the condemned prisoner he'd been so long, but like a hero, showered with flowers, gifts, admiration and honors.

The row of buses approached the camp with the huge banner saying, "Welcome Home!" Honking the horn, the bus driver cleaved a way through the massive crowd, until he finally came to a halt.

A bell began tolling when Johann disembarked from the bus, grinning from ear to ear. When the bell finished, a fire brigade band played, *"Nun danket alle Gott,"* Now thank we all our God.

The crowd went silent and listened to the music, some singing along. Johann bowed his head, biting his lips to will away the overwhelming emotions.

They had defeated death, illness, exhaustion, cold, hunger, thirst, homesickness, despair, and they had prevailed. Nobody could accuse them of being weak or whiny. In captivity they hadn't shown emotions or cried – certainly not in public.

But what happened now in the Friedland camp overwhelmed them all. It flustered even the toughest man. Johann furtively wiped his damp eyes. Glancing left and right he saw his comrades equally touched.

When the music stopped, the first couples found each other. Women wrapped their soft arms around the necks of long-lost men, and nobody could contain their tears any longer.

Women, children, men, everyone cried. Johann, too. The tears rolled down his cheeks unchecked as he witnessed the moving scenes going on around him. He walked through the crowd, looking for Lotte. He had no idea whether she'd come, whether she even knew he'd returned. Everything had happened so fast, there had been no time to write a letter.

Happy couples lay in each other's arms, kissing like there was no tomorrow. Desperate women held up signs in the air with the picture of a missing son, husband, or father and his name, asking if anyone knew about his fate. Johann turned away. Those who were still missing would never return, for they had died during the first years of hunger through 1949. One million and a half German soldiers would never make it home. The Russians had failed to register so many who'd died in the transit camps, on the marches or in the cattle trains. But who was he to shatter the hope of an old woman who still believed in a miracle?

Breathing deeply, he summoned his inner strength to continue looking for Lotte. Then he saw her. Her fiery red hair glowed in the sun. She turned her head, scanning the crowd of arrivals, and their eyes locked.

He elbowed his way through the masses, rushing toward her as fast as his feet would carry him. And finally she was in his arms, as soft and warm as he remembered her. They frantically kissed each other, making up for ten lost years and when he let go of her mouth, he saw the tears rolling down her cheeks, smearing her make-up.

"Johann." Her voice broke and once again she caught his lips in a passionate kiss.

"Lotte."

Much later, they walked across the courtyard of the camp, getting his release papers, and she said, "I knew you would come home. I've been here every single day since the first transport arrived."

"I still can't believe it," he said. "So many people."

She laughed her wonderful, glittering laugh and her eyes brightened. "You have no idea. We haven't forgotten you. For the past five years there were demonstrations, political pressure, diplomatic talks, anything you can think of, to bring all of you home."

He smiled. "I imagine you were in the middle of all of this."

"Not all, but some of it." Her happy smile warmed his heart. "I couldn't tell you in my letters. Didn't want to risk the censors knowing and giving you a hard time."

He didn't want to delve into bad memories, so he held her at arm's length and studied her appearance. She had matured; the effusiveness had left and deliberateness shaped her expression. But she was still the same person, just ten years older. "You are even more beautiful than I remember."

"I love you so much. And now we go home."

When he settled on the passenger seat in her white VW Beetle and watched her drive on the Autobahn, he thought that so much had happened in Germany while he was away. And then he laughed. "It's over. Finally."

EPILOGUE

One month later

Johann looked at the beautiful woman standing before him and he repeated the words the priest had just recited. He'd all but given up hope of marrying her, but now he stood in the church filled with friends and relatives.

"I will love you forever and I promise to protect, care, defend, and stand by you no matter what may come. In sickness and in health, until death do us part."

Lotte smiled at him and listened while the priest gave her the words to say. She repeated them to him, her voice cracking with the depth of her emotion as she uttered the final, "Till death do us part."

"I'm pleased to pronounce you husband and wife. Your love for one another has sustained you through many trials and yet you have remained true to one another. A love like yours is surely blessed from above and it gives me great pleasure to wish you the first of many congratulations on your wedding."

Johann looked at the priest and raised a brow. "Now may I kiss my bride?"

The priest smiled as those gathered to witness the momentous event chuckled behind them. "Yes, you may kiss your bride, and may you continue to kiss her for years to come."

Johann pulled Lotte into his arms and slowly lowered his lips to hers. He kissed her with all of the passion burning in his heart and felt her melt in his arms as she wrapped her slender arms around his neck and held on.

He'd been on cloud nine since his return, although he sometimes woke up in the middle of the night, panic-stricken that it was all but a dream and he was back in Russia.

But looking at her sweet face always grounded him in the new reality, one that was so different from the last decade. He still had difficulties coping and adapting. Sometimes he felt like a time traveler who'd been catapulted into the future. And other times he felt like a useless burden, a millstone around Lotte's neck.

Lotte went to work every day and he… stayed home. Unsure what to do with his life. The profession of a soldier wasn't exactly in demand right now and to tell the truth he was ready to exchange the rifle for a civilian career. Just what? Slave worker wasn't exactly a recommendation either.

Thankfully, Lotte earned enough for both of them. She

had urged him to take care of himself first, taking all the time he needed to adapt to life in freedom and decide on his career. But it undermined his sense of honor that he couldn't provide for her.

Johann finally released his new wife when the priest tapped him on the shoulder, "Son, remember this is a church."

Lotte flushed bright red and Johann grinned at her.

Life was good.

*** The End ***

AUTHOR'S NOTES

Dear Reader,

I'm so happy for Johann and Lotte, but I'm also sad, because this is the end of the War Girls series. It was originally planned as a three-book series about three German sisters and their personal struggles during the height of World War Two.

Endless Ordeal is book #10, or #12 if you count the prequel and the spin-off *Reluctant Informer*, and it's time for something new.

After giving it some thought, my next series will feature three girls (see a pattern here?) during the Berlin airlift. This was such a momentous time not only in German history, but also for the entire world. The blockade and airlift cemented the rift between the Allied powers and marked the official start of the Cold War.

If you want to stay informed about the upcoming books,

sign up for my reader's group here: https://kummerow. info/subscribe

For all of you who desire to know what happened with Johann and Lotte after they got married, let your imagination run free.

Personally, I imagine them having two children, a girl and a boy. Lotte becomes a famous lawyer hunting down the riches stolen by former Nazis.

Johann struggles for quite a while adapting to civilian life. More out of necessity than of conviction he becomes one of the first men ever to stay at home and raise their kids, freelancing as a translator from Russian to German. He refuses to set foot into the countries of the Eastern bloc and even West Berlin for the rest of his life, because he's too afraid that the Soviets for some reason will abduct him and send him back to a gulag. When he turns fifty, he finally finds his true vocation and becomes a coach for suicidal people, using his horrific experiences to help others find a reason to stay alive.

If you've read my other books you know that I always keep true to historical events. Johann Hauser is a fictional character, but the experiences he endures during his captivity are inspired by real German POWs. I have read countless testimonies from survivors, magazine articles, television reports, and non-fiction books. Articles from *Der Spiegel*, a German magazine that digitalized all their articles starting with the year 1947 and made them available for free on the internet, served as a treasure trove of information during my research. Reading authentic source material is almost like a time-travel journey back into the mindset of both families waiting at home for the return of their men and survivors who returned from captivity.

One book that impressed with the positivity the author found in his ordeal was *"und führen wohin du nicht willst"* by Helmut Gollwitzer, first published in 1954. The English title is *Unwilling Journey*, but it's out of print now. Johann's friend Helmut was inspired by this man.

The boxer Alfred was inspired by the real Oberleutnant Alfred Strunk, a well-known troublemaker. His reckless behavior was legendary from the Urals to the Siberian plains and the guards dubbed him, *"njemetzki tschort,"* the German devil. Apparently, they enjoyed giving him ever more outrageous dares to pass, which he always did. He returned with the "Last Ten Thousand."

In 1947 the Allies agreed that all prisoners of war should be sent home by the end of 1948. Maybe because of this decision the Soviet Union began convicting the prisoners for war crimes in phony mass trials to twenty-five years of forced hard labor. Only the minority of the convicted were really war criminals; the huge majority had been simple soldiers.

If you liked Endless Ordeal (or even if you didn't) I would appreciate an honest review on the retailer of your choice.

As always, I want to give thanks to everyone who helped make this book a reality. Daniela Colleo from stunning-bookcovers.com made another fantastic cover for me. My editors Tami Stark and Martin O'Hearn polished the manuscript to shine.

But my special thanks go to Ellie Midwood for revising the Russian expressions used in the book. Apart from knowing Russian she's also a fantastic author and I can't recommend her WWII books highly enough.

I may — or may not — write one very last book in the War Girl series about Rachel and her little sister Mindel in Bergen-Belsen, but my current plans are for a trilogy taking place directly after the war in Berlin. It was an exciting time, because even before the dust settled over the rubble in Berlin, the Soviets made their move to grab control over all of Berlin, Germany and eventually all of Europe.

Thank you for reading,

Marion Kummerow

From the Ashes (Book 1)

On the Brink (Book 2)

In the Skies (Book 3)

Historical Romance

Second Chance at First Love

Find all my books here:

http://www.kummerow.info

CONTACT ME

I truly appreciate you taking the time to read (and enjoy) my books. And I'd be thrilled to hear from you!
If you'd like to get in touch with me you can do so via

Twitter:
http://twitter.com/MarionKummerow

Facebook:
http://www.facebook.com/AutorinKummerow

Website
http://www.kummerow.info

Printed in Great Britain
by Amazon

42864565R00128